HOLDING HADLEIGH

PJ FIALA

RT
ROLLING THUNDER
PUBLISHING, INC.

COPYRIGHT

Printed in the United States of America

First published 2021

Fiala, PJ

HOLDING HADLEIGH / PJ Fiala

p. cm.

1. Romance—Fiction. 2. Romance—Suspense. 3. Romance - Military

I. Title – HOLDING HADLEIGH

ISBN: 978-1-942618-59-1

DEDICATION

I've had so many wonderful people come into my life and I want you all to know how much I appreciate it. From each and every reader who takes the time out of their days to read my stories and leave reviews, thank you.

My beautiful, smart and fun Road Queens, who play games with me, post fun memes, keep the conversation rolling and help me create these captivating characters, places, businesses and more. Thank you ladies for your ideas, support and love. The following characters and places were created by:

Hadleigh Watterson - Jo West

Hadleigh's brother - Holden - Barb Keller

Hadleigh's father - Lisa Rolape Courter

Hadleigh's mother - Claire - Pat Elliott

Lucy Carlisle - Karen Cranford LeBeau

Hadleigh's cousin - Hannah - Beckie Johnson Lowe

Hadleigh's aunt - Marnie - Kerry Harteker

Donovan Keach - Georgine Wood - (Donovan) Kim Kurtz (Keach)

Neighborhood Cafe - Ramona Pierce

Station Street - Jo West
Autumn Lynn - Judy Hamilton
Brent Jennings - Denise Scott
Top End Automotive - Debbie Zsidai
The Dip n' Twist - Christy Seiple
Reggie's on the Lake - Kari Wolff
Jenn Owens - Karen Cranford LeBeau
Leslie Knot - Pat Elliott
Haylie Tomms - Cindy Pearson

A very special thank you to April Bennett and Judy Rosen
my amazing editors!

This gorgeous cover was designed by Stacy Garcia,
Graphics by Stacy.

Photo image on the cover purchased from Eric McKinney
at 612 Photograhy.

Last but not least, my family for the love and sacrifices
they have made and continue to make to help me achieve
this dream, especially my husband and best friend, Gene.
Words can never express how much you mean to me.
To our veterans and current serving members of our
armed forces, police and fire departments, thank you
ladies and gentlemen for your hard work and sacrifices;
it's with gratitude and thankfulness that I mention you in
this forward.

BLURB

Read the prequel to RAPTOR - RAPTOR Rising here.

A RAPTOR operative on a mission.

A social worker with unfaltering compassion.

And the competition that sparks desire.....

Former Army Ranger Donovan Keach can't stand the scum that threatens children. Determined to take down an online pedophile, he'll stop at nothing until the criminal is locked up for good. But when he encounters a sexy, but nosy social worker, he suspects foul play.

Hadleigh Watterson will do anything to protect innocent children. While gathering evidence during a case study, Donovan sidetracks her plan. She's ready to barrel in and take down the vermin muddying the innocent. Donovan has other plans. With an intense attraction building between them, teaming up is their only option. Can

Donovan uncover the criminal while holding on to Hadleigh for good?

***

Let's stay in contact, join my newsletter so I can let you know about new releases, sales, promotions and more. https://www.subscribepage.com/pjfialafm

GLOSSARY

Read the prequel to RAPTOR - RAPTOR Rising here.

A Note from Emersyn Copeland:

Founder of RAPTOR (Revenge And Protect Team Operation Recovery).

I was wounded when my convoy hit an IED and retrained through OLA (Operation Live Again) to perform useful services for the military; mainly locating missing children. Empowered by the work but frustrated by governmental limitations, I contacted my father Dane Copeland and my Uncle Gaige Vickers, GHOST's leader, to form a covert group not restricted by governmental regulations, consisting of highly trained post military men and women with injuries and disabilities. Our offices are housed on the GHOST compound. I divided RAPTOR into three teams of expertly trained individuals who were selected for their specific abilities. Let me introduce you to the Teams.

Team Alpha: Recon and Recovery:

Diego Josephs: Former Army Recon expert. Friend of GHOST Josh Masters. Recent retraining for OLR (Operation Live Again). Demonstrative and possessive, he is a team player battling PTSD.

Ted: Diego's Therapy and service dog. A mix of black lab and Newfoundland.

Donovan "Van" Keach aka the "Reformer": Completed OLR with Emersyn. Blinded in his left eye during a military operation. Out spoken, opinionated, daredevil with a strong belief in service and a mission for justice no matter the risk.

Charlesia "Charly" Sampson: A friend of Emersyn's Aunt Sophie. Medically discharged after she lost her left arm at the elbow during a mission in Afghanistan. Tough adaptable, independent sarcastic, and determined but self-conscious of her appearance. Excels in disarming and getting people to trust her and ferreting out information.

Team Bravo: Cyber Intelligence:

Piper Dillon: Attractive and energetic with a ready smile but all business. Expert computer hacker, communications device expert and internet guru.

Caiden Marx: Strong and independent, Caiden suffered lung damage while serving due to an explosion and fire. He struggles to breathe and can't take on energetic tasks but excels on Team Bravo and has unique hacker abilities.

Deacon Smythe: Deacon has a ready smile and is always happy but takes his job seriously. He's an expert on computers and communications.

Team Charlie, Special Ops:

Falcon Montgomery: Son of Ford Montgomery, a GHOST team member, Falcon lost hearing in his right ear. Growing up with Ford, Falcon is a natural in special ops, and willing to go the extra mile to get the job done.

Creed Rowan: Former SEAL, well rounded in terms of skill, Creed's specialties are explosives and swimming. His abilities take him places others don't dare go.

Emersyn Copeland: Daughter of GHOST founder, Dane Copeland and niece to current GHOST owner, Gaige Vickers, Emersyn's strengths are in business and extracting her staff member's special talents. But, she's equally good at ferreting out suspects' deep dark secrets.

House Staff:

Sheldon Daniels, Cook: Former military, Marine. Friend of GHOST's house keeper and cook Mrs. James. Demands order in his kitchen, punctuality and the keeper of all secrets, bonus he's a damned good cook.

Shioban O'Hearn, Housekeeper: Sassy mid- thirties housekeeper. Loves the thrill of working with badasses, but doesn't let herself get walked on.

1

Donovan pocketed his phone, tucked his 9mm into his waistband holster, and swiped his wallet from his dresser top. Walking from his bedroom, to the door of his apartment inside the RAPTOR complex, he nabbed his keys from the hook hanging by the door and stepped into the hall. Taking long strides to the elevator a door closed at the end of the hall. Turning he nodded when Diego and his therapy dog, Ted, caught up to him.

"On your way to investigate the house you think Marco48 is operating from?"

"Yeah. I've been after this guy for months. I can't believe I'm finally going to make contact."

"Want company?"

"Yeah, but Charly's coming with me. No offense, but she's better looking than you are. And Ted takes up the whole backseat."

Ted barked and Van chuckled. "Sorry bud, but it's the truth."

Diego laughed. "Ignore him Ted, he's not that great of company when he's on the trail anyway."

Van laughed. "Fuck off."

The elevator doors opened and Diego stepped in first with Ted, laughing as he entered. Van stepped in and pushed the button for the lower level where their conference room and offices were located; although calling them offices was a bit formal. It was a large room where they each had a desk set up with short walls around each desk for minimal privacy. Not that they needed it. Everyone here knew what everyone else was working on. Whenever back up or assistance was needed, no one had to be brought up to speed on anything.

Van's stomach was a bit tense and right now he wished he hadn't eaten so much for lunch. Since he wasn't sure how long he'd have to sit in his car today while he watched the house he believed Marco48 operated from, he ate a large breakfast so he wouldn't get hungry. Now, lunch sat like a rock and he regretted his decision.

Letting out a long slow breath to calm his nerves, he watched the doors to the elevator as if that would speed things up.

Diego nudged him. "It's all good Van. You've got this."

Van nodded, "Yeah, but just when I let myself think that, something will go wrong. So, I keep running over all the possible scenarios in my mind."

"That's because you're a great operative. And, Charly has an eagle eye, so don't for one minute doubt yourself on the vision front. Believe in yourself, everyone else here does."

"I just want this guy. Bad."

Diego laughed. "You'll get him."

"Thanks. I could use your help though. Can you go through the reports Cyber ran on Marco48? Mostly, are there any red flags? Do you see any consistencies in his patterns I haven't noticed? You're much better at that stuff than I am."

"You got it. I'll message you when I have something."

The elevator doors opened and they walked to the conference room. In his head, Van often called this room Mission Control. It was the hub of the complex, the place where all the information was disseminated and forwarded. It's where they met to discuss their missions and where they viewed information. It was the most exciting place to be.

Opening the conference room door, he stepped into the activity and his heartbeat increased. His boss, Emersyn Copeland, sat across the room at her desk, engrossed in whatever she was looking at on her computer while the large printer to her right was in the process of printing something.

To his right was a bank of computers and a plethora of computer monitors hanging on the wall. Someone from their cyber team, Team Bravo, was always manning their computers. They had all sorts of online connections being made, which is how he got hooked up with Marco48. Piper, one of Team Bravo's computer specialists made contact, pretending to be a little boy looking for a sugar daddy. As soon as Marco48 communicated with her, she handed him off to Donovan, who took it from there while Piper and the others, Caiden and Deacon, continued looking for pervs to make contact with. Sometimes they went out in the field, but other times they handed those guys off to the other teams. Diego, Donovan, and Charlesia, were Team Alpha and Emmy, Falcon, and Creed were Team Charlie. Piper looked over her shoulder, "Hey Van, I've got the packet all loaded into the system on Marco48, including the maps to the house."

She tapped her keyboard and soon a map was shown on the screen in front of her. "This is the house. It's right in Lynyrd Station, Van." She pointed. "This is the view across the street. There's a little coffee shop right here...Neighborhood Café." She moved the map on the screen and showed him the parking lot. "You should be able to see the house perfectly from the coffee shop parking lot."

"What are the fucking odds? "

"Right?"

"Any activity?"

"Yeah." She tapped a few more times and on another screen a video began playing. Piper zoomed in. "This woman right here," she pointed to a woman walking up to the house with long dark blonde hair, wearing nude-colored heels, blue jeans, and a white blouse looked around the street suspiciously before knocking. She continued to look around the street until the door opened.

Unable to see who opened the door, the woman entered the house and just a few minutes later, exited with a younger boy, no more than five years old.

"Do you know who that is?"

Piper shook her head. "Not yet. I haven't been able to identify her. But I'm still working on it. My camera is too far away to get enough of her features to be able to set up facial recognition. I'll have someone go out and move the camera later today, we're working out the logistics right now."

"Okay. Did she bring the boy back to the house?"

"Yeah, but here's what's weird, she brought him back then left with another child. A girl, who is a little bit older."

Piper sped up the video and the woman appeared again on camera bringing the little boy back to the house, entering the front door, then exiting a few minutes later with a little girl. By the looks of the girl, she was around eight or nine years old.

"Who are the kids?"

"I don't know. I'm running the owner of the house right now to see who owns it. Real estate records are shady on this one. Its last three owners have been companies, all LLCs.

"Thanks Piper. As soon as Charly gets down here, we're off."

The door opened and Charly entered the room. "I'm right here and raring to go."

Charly was a vivacious blonde knockout with light blue eyes, perfect teeth, clear complexion, a narrow waist, and a quick wit. She'd been injured during active duty when her unit engaged in fire with insurgents and her left arm was hit with a round of bullets, shattering her bones. The arm had to be amputated from the elbow down, but she had a prosthetic arm in its place and she managed it quite well.

"Okay then, we're ready here."

Emmy walked toward them. "We just got the okay for payment on this one. Guess who's footing the bill?"

Van looked into Emmy's dark brown eyes. "The smile on your face tells me you're happy about this, so let me ask, is it something you've been working on for a while?"

"Yes."

It was impossible not to return her smile. "Dare I say we're getting paid by the government on this one?"

"You should dare. Not only just the nameless faceless government but by none other than the Federal Bureau of Protection for Families and Children."

Charly's eyes rounded. "That's the agency that was paying for Operation Live Again."

"Correct. We finally got our foot in the door. Things are looking up."

Van chuckled. "I'll bet if Sergeant Dildo knew this, he'd spit up a lung."

Emmy laughed. "I hope that asshole does find out."

Charly clapped her hands together. "Does this mean we have a bigger budget?"

"Yes, it means just that. We'll be able to get more cameras and more equipment now. It means a lot of good things to come. Not only for this job, but they'll put us on retainer for three to five years. To get the five-year commitment from them, we need to get Marco48 and anyone else he's working with. If we can do it under budget, even better. We need to prove to the Bureau this is where their money is better spent."

Van nodded, "We're on it."

Van turned to walk out of Mission Control and looked over at Diego, already pouring through the reports for him. "Thanks Diego." He called out as they exited. Diego never looked up. He was one of the best.

2

Waking early, Hadleigh stumbled to the kitchen and turned the stove on under her tea kettle, already filled and ready for this morning. She wasn't a morning person. Standing at the back window of her home she watched the birds play around the freshly bloomed flowers in her landscaping, nipping at the dampened ground and the worms within.

A beautiful cardinal landed on the post of the bird feeder, its ever-watchful eyes searching the area for predators before partaking of its morning meal.

The whistle in her tea kettle began to sound. Wrapping a potholder around the handle, she poured the hot water into her cup, added her favorite peppermint tea bag, and blankly stared into her cup as the steam rose and the water turned dark.

Today she had a full load. Being a social worker was all she'd ever wanted to be growing up. But then, she didn't know the pressures of the job. In her child's mind she would be helping those who needed help the most—children. And she was doing that. Helping. She hoped so anyway. But it was the unknown that traumatized her sleep at night. What happened to these kids when they aged out of the system? It was impossible to keep track of all of them and frankly, many of them had found good homes to be raised in. They learned discipline, manners, great study habits, and got good grades. Many of them. But, those others. The ones who had the worst starts in life and had developed those bad habits. Bad attitudes. Bad everything. Mostly out of a sense of self-defense. Those kids were destined for a hard life. That's what kept her awake at night. Could she have done more? Could she have found a better placement for them that would have offered them more of the essentials to get by in life? Did she miss signs? Did she understand all their needs?

She tried. She really tried. In the past year she decided to change how she approached her job. Her mentor, Lucy Carlisle, told her to focus on the families she was placing the kids with. If you found the right family, decent people and fostering for the right reasons, you'd have better placements and the kids thrived. So now, as she entered the homes of her placed children, she focused more on the family, the child's demeanor with the family around, and the child outside of the family. She was still transitioning to the new method. Today, she had five appointments. Of these five, two were with her new approach.

Declaring her tea fully steeped, she took a sip and closed her eyes as the warm liquid slid down her throat. Yeah —nice.

After turning on the shower to warm, Hadleigh set her cup on the dresser and selected her clothing for today's appointments. A pair of jeans, thank God she could wear jeans at work, a soft green blouse, and her favorite nude-colored sandals. Perfect.

Feeling fresh and ready to tackle the day after her shower, Hadleigh dried her long hair, letting the natural wave do its thing before finishing her cup of tea, then out the door she went. Today would be a good day, she could feel it.

The sun was shining, the air dry and warm, and all things looked promising.

Five hours later, Hadleigh pulled into the driveway of her fifth and final home visit for the day. She pulled her file from the file organizer on the passenger floor and tucked it in her over-large canvas bag.

She'd been pleasantly surprised at how well her visits had gone today and hoped this one would be just as good as the others.

Walking up to the house, she enjoyed the wonderful aroma of coffee from the shop across the street. They roasted and ground their own coffee beans and when they did, the delicious smells that came from the vents made her mouth water. She loved the smell of coffee, but drank tea. What did that say about her?

The stone steps of the Connert home were swept clean. The small front yard was mowed, but nothing of beauty or that feeling of home spoke to her. Some people didn't understand how important a few well-placed flowers could be. This street, one off of Main Street, was filled with narrow brick two-story homes of largely the same style. Most of them built more than seventy-five years ago, most of them kept in reasonable repair. Luckily, Lynyrd Station was small enough that homeowners tried to keep their properties neat. Station Street had a newly activated neighborhood revitalization committee, which is how the coffee shop ended up across the road. They ran a campaign to bring only five businesses to this block in an effort to remodel some of the older homes that had fallen into disrepair. The coffee shop was the first to move in and as soon as they'd finished their project, suddenly there was a list of businesses vying for position here. A flower shop was opening in a week next to the coffee shop and two doors down from the Connert home, a furniture maker and repair shop was moving in later this year after the home they purchased was complete. A side bonus had been that the teenagers on this street were given jobs in these businesses and they didn't have travel costs. Win-win.

Taking one more deep breath, she knocked on the door to the Connert home and mentally checked her list of things to watch for. The clicking of the locks turning captured her attention and the door cracked open. The sweet face of the eight-year-old girl she'd placed here last month, Autumn Lynn, appeared in the crack of space between the door and the jamb.

"Hi Autumn, it's Hadleigh Watterson, your social worker. We have an appointment today."

Autumn turned to look into the house then with sullen brown eyes she looked directly at Hadleigh and shook her head.

"Why are you shaking your head, Autumn. We have an appointment. Are Bethany or Melvyn Connert home?"

"Let her in Autumn. She's correct, we have an appointment." A woman's voice said from down a hallway.

Autumn opened the door and stepped back. Hadleigh's eyes immediately assessed Autumn. Her blonde hair was clean and combed. It had been cut into a short bob, which was adorable on her and made her brown eyes seem much larger than they were. She was a stunning girl. Her lips seemed a tad pink and Hadleigh stared at them for a few beats.

"Are you wearing lipstick?"

"Just a little." Autumn mumbled.

"But you're only eight."

Bethany Connert came bustling down the hallway with a ten-month old boy on her hip, who had clearly just finished eating.

"Come in Ms. Watterson. I'm sorry, we got a bit of a late start this morning and I was just finishing up feeding Henry."

Bethany stepped back into the living room to give Hadleigh room to enter and smiled brightly, though she seemed a tad frazzled.

"If you need to finish feeding Henry, I can visit with Autumn for a bit to give you the time."

Bethany looked at Henry and smiled, "Are you still hungry little one?"

Henry shook his blonde head and reached for Autumn, who took him from Bethany and walked to the sofa with him. Pulling some toys from a basket under the coffee table, Autumn sat and played with Henry.

Bethany smiled, "She's good with him."

"That's wonderful."

Wiping her hands on the front of the house frock she wore, Bethany smiled. "Can I get you some coffee or tea?"

Hadleigh couldn't stop looking at Autumn's lips. She also seemed more sullen today than usual and this was concerning.

"No thank you, I'm fine. I'd like to start by visiting with Autumn for a few minutes. I'd like to take a little walk."

Bethany smiled at Autumn, "Go get your shoes, love, Ms. Watterson wants to go for a little walk and chat."

3

That was her, the same woman as the one in the video.

"Charly, when was the video taken that Piper showed us today?"

Charly tapped on the laptop on her knees and opened up the video. "Looks like two weeks ago."

Van watched the pretty woman walk up to the home and look around. She seemed to assess the area or was she making sure no one was watching her? In his job, he'd learned to be suspicious of everyone. After all, even their sergeant in Operation Live Again was dirty and he was supposed to be operating with them. You just never knew people and what their own motivations were for anything.

The door cracked open and the woman talked to someone for a few moments before entering the house, though he couldn't see who she spoke with. Looking down the street both ways, Van assessed the street himself. Traffic was minor, most of it was foot traffic as folks seemed to appreciate the coffee shop here in their neighborhood. Mostly groups of two and three women, out for their daily walk, who stopped in and bought a coffee to go, and there was a car or two that had pulled up. One had a man in a suit in it, the other a local painter or tradesman who stopped in and left a few moments later with a coffee cup and a white bag of something to eat.

The door to the house opened and out stepped the woman with a young girl who looked to be around seven or eight. They exited the yard and turned left to walk away from the coffee shop and his line of sight. Tempted to follow on foot Van mulled over what he should do when Charly said, "I think I'll take a walk."

Before he could respond, she'd hopped from his SUV and was walking toward the woman and little girl. Van continued to watch the house. About fifteen minutes later, a woman stepped out of the house carrying a little boy, not quite a year old. After she descended the three porch steps, she walked to the side of the house where a garage stood at the back of the property. Van lost sight of her for a few moments, then the woman emerged pulling the little guy in a wagon.

He watched them disappear down the street before turning his head to see the woman he'd seen earlier walking back to the house with the little girl, Charly was on the opposite side of the street coming toward the car.

The little girl seemed upset, the woman seemed frustrated, and now his curiosity was definitely piqued.

Charly got into the car and watched the pair with Van for a moment before saying anything.

"The only thing I could hear was the woman asking the girl about the lipstick she was wearing. The girl clammed right up and didn't want to discuss it and then they noticed me walking behind them. They stopped to wait for me to pass them and I didn't want to seem as though I was eavesdropping, so I moved to the opposite side of the street. I should have had a microphone on, that's for sure."

"So you can't figure out what's going on with the kids?"

"No, did you see anything?"

"Yes, a woman walked out of the house a few minutes ago with a little boy, put him in a wagon and walked that way..." He pointed in the direction they walked. The woman and the little girl were now walking up the three steps to the front door and the young girl seemed hesitant. The woman then sat down on the top step and patted the area next to her by way of invitation.

Van stared at them. "The video showed that one there..." He pointed to the woman, "walking out of the house with a five-year-old boy last week. The boy the woman came out with was much younger. So, where did that little boy go? Or is he in the house with someone else?"

The young girl sat down next to the woman, tucked her hands in her lap, and bent her head down.

A young boy approached the house and froze when he saw them sitting on the steps. The woman looked up and Van could see her face clearly. She seemed surprised to see the boy and stood to walk toward him. As she neared, the boy took off running and the woman started after him, then stopped and watched as the young girl went into the house.

Turning to follow the girl into the house, Van sat quietly as his eyes moved from the front of the house, to the direction the boy ran, to the direction the woman had walked, and was now more confused than ever.

"What the hell do you make of any of this?"

Charly let out a long breath. "I simply don't have a clue."

Checking his phone for any texts from Piper or any of Team Bravo on the internet searches they were still doing, his disappointment intensified when he saw nothing.

"My gut tells me there's something amiss here. I'm to meet Marco48 in three days. We need cameras set up around here to monitor more of the comings and goings and I'd like some in the back by the garage area as well."

"I agree. I wonder how well some of the neighbors know what's happening in this house, or at least, who owns it or lives in it?"

"I think that's our next job. Which side of the street do you want to take?"

Charly giggled, "I'll take the south side. Meet you back here in an hour?"

"Yep. Piper will have video on the house and when the woman leaves and who with. In the meantime, I got her license plate number and sent that in to Piper. We'll find out who she is soon enough."

4

H adleigh looked around the living room and didn't see Bethany or Henry anywhere. "Do you know where I might find Bethany?"

Autumn looked around, then walked to the back of the house; Hadleigh followed her to the kitchen. They walked through the dining room before reaching the kitchen. Autumn turned and shrugged.

"She may have taken Henry for a walk. Brent wants quiet during some parts of the day."

Hadleigh's brows furrowed. "Who's Brent?"

Autumn looked at the floor and mumbled. "Ms. Connert's brother."

"Is he living here now?"

Autumn shook her head. "No, he's just staying here for a little while."

"Where's Mr. Connert?"

"At work."

The front door opened and Bethany Connert entered the house carrying a squirmy Henry. Laughing, she gently set him on the floor and he immediately crawled to the toy basket. Bethany laughed and looked at the two of them.

"Did you have a nice visit?"

Hadleigh looked down at Autumn who nodded but said nothing. Looking at Bethany again Hadleigh smiled. "Autumn's a bit quiet today."

"Yes, she's been that way for the past couple of days. I've been asking if she's feeling okay and she tells me yes."

Hadleigh touched Autumn's shoulder. The little girl's eyes looked up at her and she could just tell something was wrong. Kneeling down she looked Autumn in the eye on her level. "If there is anything wrong, you can tell me. If there is anything you are struggling with, you can tell me."

Hadleigh pulled her business card from her back pocket. She handed one to Autumn, "You can call me anytime. Okay?"

Autumn nodded and Hadleigh stood and handed Bethany a card as well.

"You likely already have this, but here's my card again. Anytime you need anything please let me know."

"Thank you, Ms. Watterson."

"Hadleigh, please."

Bethany folded her hands together and cleared her throat. "Have you heard anything about how Donny is? I miss that little boy so much. He was such a cuddler."

Hadleigh smiled at Bethany, she was a great foster parent and she loved her kids, all of them. Donny had been with them for about a year, but then had been adopted just this week.

"I don't have any follow up on him yet, but I promise to let you know."

Looking down at Autumn again Hadleigh asked, "Is that why you're so sad Autumn? Do you miss Donny?"

Autumn nodded and tears sprang to her eyes.

Bethany walked to Autumn and knelt in front of her, "Oh, honey, I'm so sorry. I've been so wrapped up in my own grief I didn't even think that you missed him as well. Please forgive my self-absorption."

Autumn mumbled, "It's okay."

Taking a deep breath, Hadleigh felt relieved. Then she felt embarrassed that she hadn't thought about Donny's leaving as making Autumn sad. She had to remember to watch the family unit as a whole and that included when children came and went. Of course, it would leave a void, especially with the younger ones.

"Bethany, Autumn mentioned that your brother is staying here. Is he here now?"

Bethany looked up at her then stood. "He's still sleeping. He's a bit of a night owl. That's why I take the kids out for a walk or to the park during the day, so he can sleep. It's easier on all of us."

"Sure. I'd like to meet him."

The sounds of someone moving around upstairs made Hadleigh look up at the ceiling. The bathroom door closed and Bethany said, "He'll be down in a bit it seems."

"That's great. Is he staying here for an extended period?"

"No, he's just here for three weeks. He travels around for his job and he had a little break so he came to visit. I don't get to see him much."

"It's nice that he could come and visit, but you need to let my office know when you have someone else staying in close proximity to the children."

Bethany's hand rose to her mouth and her eyes rounded. "Oh, I'm so sorry. He just got here a week ago and in all the excitement, I completely forgot."

"It's okay. Just a reminder that we need to know. I'll need to see his room and where he's staying in proximity to the children."

"Oh, sure."

Footsteps were heard on the stairs and a man came around the corner. Hadleigh could see him from her vantage point, it was a straight shot from the kitchen in the back of the house, through the dining room to the living room. Most of these row type houses were designed that way.

His dark hair was messed up, he was clothed in dark blue sweatpants, a light blue t-shirt, and his feet were bare.

When he entered the room, his eyes locked on Hadleigh's and she thought he was very handsome with his short hair on the sides and a bit longer on top. Even tousled it was attractive. He had a day's growth of facial hair and his eyes were a crisp light blue. He seemed fit and around six feet tall and she didn't get any creepy vibes from him.

"Here he is. Ms. Hadleigh Watterson this is my brother, Brent Jennings. Brent, this is Hadleigh, she's the social worker who placed Autumn and Henry and Donny, before them, with us."

Hadleigh continued her eye contact and so did Brent. He reached forward with his right hand and she grasped it in a firm handshake.

"It's nice to meet you, Brent. I understand you travel quite a bit for your job. What do you do for a living?"

He smiled and she thought he was incredibly attractive. "I'm a location scout for a movie studio. I travel around looking at all the best places, and sometimes some of the worst, depending on the movie."

"Wow, that sounds very interesting."

"It is."

"So, part of my job is that I need to see where you're staying while you're here. I'm sorry I didn't have time to give you notice, but this is a surprise to me."

He shrugged and held his hand out toward the stairs. "No worries, feel free to look around."

Bethany turned and walked toward the stairs, "I can show you Hadleigh, follow me."

Hadleigh followed Bethany to the staircase and then up to the second floor. Leaning over the railing she looked through to the kitchen and saw Autumn looking up at Brent and smiling. That had been the first time she'd smiled since Hadleigh had gotten here today.

At the top of the stairs Bethany pointed to the first door on the left, "This is our bedroom. You're welcome to look in."

The door was open, so Hadleigh looked inside and saw a neat and tidy room; bed made, curtains open, and the furniture polished and tidy.

"Across the hall here is where Henry sleeps."

Bethany opened the door to Henry's room and she saw a sweet little baby's room painted a light yellow with cute children's pictures on the walls in primary colors.

"You keep the house so neat and clean Bethany. So many homes are not this well-kept."

Bethany's cheeks flushed. "Thank you. I take pride in my home and since Melvyn and I couldn't have our own children, having these foster children here has certainly filled a void."

Bethany walked to the bedroom next to Henry's and opened the door to a nice sunny room painted the same soft yellow as Henry's room but with more mature art on the walls. "This is Autumn's room."

"It's very inviting." Hadleigh looked around and didn't see anything out of place. "Is Autumn still doing her schooling on-line?"

"Yes, she logs in each morning and gets her lessons. Once Mel gets home tonight, he'll help Autumn with her homework while I get Henry fed and ready for bed."

Bethany walked across the hall. The door was left open and the bed unmade. Bethany walked in to begin making the bed. "My brother didn't get my neatness gene I'm afraid."

The room wasn't dirty, just messy. The bed unmade, an open suitcase on the floor in front of the closet, and some clothing strewn across the chair in the corner.

"It's fine Bethany, I just needed to see it."

They stepped into the hall and Hadleigh noticed another door at the end of the hall. "Whose room is that one?"

"Oh, it's no one's room. We use it for storage now."

"May I see it?"

"Of course."

Bethany walked to the door and opened it. It was dark so she flicked the light switch on to illuminate the room. Shelves on two of the walls held neatly placed boxes and two chairs were along the far wall. The closed curtains were a deep burgundy color. No bed, no dresser.

"Okay, thank you for showing me." Hadleigh turned to leave but saw something sticking out from under the pulled curtain. Walking to the window, she pulled the curtain back to see a camera on a tripod.

"What's this for?"

5

Donovan left the light tan brick house next to the Connert house without any additional information. The Connerts were a quiet family who kept to themselves. They had children, though those changed here and there and it wasn't uncommon to see a new face leaving their house at any given time. They stayed to themselves, kept their lawn mowed, didn't play loud music; the usual things neighbors cared about.

He saw Charly walking to his SUV and realized she'd struck out as well. Looking both ways, he stepped into the street and met her at the SUV.

Opening the driver's door and sliding inside he stared at the Connert house. "Get anything?"

"No."

"Me neither."

Charly's phone received a text and she looked at the screen.

"Piper has information on the car the leggy blonde got out of."

Van turned his head to look at Charly only to find her smiling at him. "You have to admit, she's gorgeous."

"I don't have to admit anything."

Charly scoffed and continued reading the texts that continued to populate on her phone.

"So her name is Hadleigh Watterson. I have an address on her. Should we do a drive-by and see what her situation is?"

"I guess we can do that. There's not much going on here and I haven't gotten an email today from Marco48. It's a bit unusual since he's been emailing daily."

"What do you make of that?"

"He thinks he's making me sweat."

"Ah, okay, to make sure you really want to meet him to see if he's primed you correctly?"

"Yep. So that means..." Van pulled his phone from the cup holder of his vehicle and began typing out an email. "Time to look desperate."

I haven't heard from you today. I hope everything is okay. I still want to meet you. Are you still going to meet me on Thurs.? Please say yes. Ricky."

After sending the email he set his phone in the cup holder once more, then started his vehicle.

"May as well GPS Hadleigh's address and we'll see where she lives and if there's anything going on there."

Charly's fingers raced over the keys on her phone. This was especially impressive since she typed with one hand. He always marveled at how she'd adapted from losing her arm. He still felt like he struggled with the lost vision in his left eye. It took him two different times to pass his driver's test and he was bitter about that. "Okay, turn right out of the parking lot here."

Charly navigated their way to Hadleigh Watterson's address and he played over in his mind what her involvement was. A few things came to mind and none of them were good.

Charly spoke first, "You know she's likely a social worker or something."

"Why do you say that? I don't know any social workers who go to people's homes and leave with a child one after another. She's more likely a trafficker bringing kids by for grooming."

"You're a cynic."

"I've good reason to be a cynic and so have you."

Charly shrugged. "I don't want to think like that. There are still good people in the world, we just happen to always have to deal with the bad ones."

Van didn't respond because, frankly, he didn't want to get into an argument with Charly.

"Okay, left at the next street, then it's the second house on the left."

He navigated the turns and slowed as they drove past Hadleigh Watterson's home. A younger man, or perhaps a teenager, left via the front door. He had a bit of a skip in his step as he walked to the street and jumped into a car approximately ten years old. Van navigated his SUV past the car and Charly took a good look at the male inside.

"He looks young, about sixteen I'd say. He was counting money."

Van's jaw clenched. "She's grooming kids."

"We don't know yet."

Van took a deep breath and let it out slowly as he navigated the street Watterson's house was on. The houses were smaller, around 1,400–1,600 square feet, small lots and the trees and shrubs were all small. So, not an old neighborhood. Most of the garage doors were closed and the homes looked buttoned up for the day; likely most of the residents worked during the day.

Nearing the end of the street, he pulled into a driveway and began to back out when he saw the kid in the car in front of Watterson's house complete a U-turn and screech his tires on the way out of the neighborhood.

As he put his SUV in drive, he saw Watterson's car turn onto the street. He drove slowly, hoping to see some activity and watch her for a bit.

She pulled into her driveway and the garage door slowly opened as she sat in her car waiting for it to rise. Once completely up, she slowly drove her car inside, but did not lower the door. She opened her car door and stepped from inside, Charly was right, she did have long legs. They were encased in denim today, but he figured they were phenomenal legs. She walked toward the end of the driveway and stepped onto the street. Looking both ways she tossed her head saucily, her long blonde hair blew behind her shoulders and the light breeze in the air lifted tiny wayward strands as she stopped in front of a bank of mailboxes and opened the second box in from the right.

Pulling mail from the box, she sifted through it, then looked up as they approached her.

"You ready?" he asked Charly.

"Yep."

Charly rolled her window down and Van stopped his SUV alongside the blonde beauty at the mailboxes.

"Hi, my husband and I were hoping to find a house for sale in this neighborhood. You don't happen to know of any, do you?"

She smiled and Van couldn't stop staring, she was a beautiful woman. Too bad she was a pedophile.

6

H adleigh stared at the camera, partially hidden but likely supposed to be fully hidden and her blood ran cold.

Staring at the camera, which had it been pointing at the window, she'd have wondered if someone was taking pictures of the house next door, but since it was facing the empty room, her suspicious mind ran a reel of horror movies through her head.

"Oh, dear, I'm not sure what that's doing in here." Bethany stammered.

"Why is it set up and then hidden?"

Bethany walked forward and stared at the camera along with Hadleigh. Neither of them touched it but Hadleigh stepped around to peer at the back of it and saw that it was digital. She had no right to touch the camera and she had no right to confiscate it. But her hackles reared up and her shoulders stiffened.

"I don't know. I simply don't know." Bethany answered.

"Have you seen it before? Is it yours? Melvyn's? Brent's?"

She turned to watch Bethany's face and the bewilderment on it told her she was either a great actress or she didn't know about the camera in here.

"I've never seen it before. We don't use this room for anything except storage. I don't know who would have had it set up."

Hadleigh looked at the floor in the room. The old wooden floors were clean, no dust on it as you'd expect a storage room to have.

"Do you clean this room, Bethany?"

"Not generally. If I bring things up here to store and notice it needs a dusting or vacuuming I will, but otherwise I generally don't clean this room."

Taking a look at the shelves, Hadleigh looked at the neatly stacked boxes and totes on the shelves and noted that all were clearly labeled and categorized by holiday. Christmas. Easter. Halloween. Summer. Fourth of July. Then there were other totes, smaller in size that were labeled Family Pictures. Mom's things. Crafts. Needlepoint. None of them looked suspicious or as though they'd been moved in a while. Walking along the shelves, she noticed a piece of red fabric on top of the totes just above her head.

"What's this?"

She gave it a little tug and more material pulled down. It was a large bed sheet in deep red and fastened to the wall above the shelves. As she tugged it down, she noted that it fell to the floor and when spread out, would be a perfect backdrop for a photo. Her stomach lurched.

"Bethany." She whispered her name and turned to face the white-faced woman who looked as shocked as Hadleigh felt. "I don't...I'm not sure...I don't know who did this." She touched the edge of the fabric with her fingers and her eyes glistened with tears.

Bethany slowly lifted the sheet and began clumsily folding it to put it back where it had been resting. Her fingers shook slightly but Hadleigh was unable to help her. Her feet felt frozen to the floor; she worried that if she moved she'd lose the little bit of food she'd eaten today.

Bethany reached up and tucked the sheet onto the totes above her head then slowly turned to face Hadleigh. "I'll find out who is taking pictures and of what and let you know."

Hadleigh finally found her voice after a short silence. "I have to write a report."

Bethany burst into tears. "Please don't take the children from me."

"It's my job to make sure they're safe."

"They are safe. I keep them safe."

"Why is Autumn wearing lipstick today?"

Bethany blinked a few times and swiped at the tears that had fallen.

"What do you mean?"

"Bethany, Autumn is wearing pink lipstick. Do you know where she got it or why an eight-year-old girl is wearing pink lipstick? Didn't you notice?"

Bethany took a deep breath, squared her shoulders and stared directly at Hadleigh. The change that came over her was immediate and indifferent.

"I have to go and check on Henry and Autumn. Is there anything else you need from me today Ms. Watterson?"

She was being dismissed. What the ever-loving fu...

"No Bethany, that will be all for today."

She turned and walked out of the room, proud that she didn't lose her shit just now. There was something nefarious going on in this house and, at first, she didn't think Bethany knew anything about it, but her sudden change in demeanor now raised the hairs on the back of her neck. She'd never experienced anything like this and she needed assistance in dealing with it from someone more experienced than she. Even with weak knees she managed to navigate the steps to the main level of the house and at the bottom she turned to walk to the back of the house where Autumn was still with Brent, but Bethany nicely said, "I'll tell Autumn you had to leave, Ms. Watterson."

Hadleigh stopped and looked Bethany square in the eyes, leaving no uncertainty that she indeed would be writing a report and having this looked into, but nodded and replied, "Thank you. I'll be in touch soon."

Bethany's jaw tightened. That was it though. The woman had just changed from a sweet kindly mommy to someone else. Firm. Strong. Fierce. Likely afraid now that she'd lose the kids and never be able to foster again, she was going to protect what was hers right now.

That gave Hadleigh more cause for concern. This could be a very bad situation. Leaving the house, she inhaled deeply as the fresh breeze from outside and the robust aroma from the Neighborhood Cafe wrapped itself around her. She slowly walked to her car, opened the driver's door but froze. Tossing her file on the Connerts into the passenger seat, she walked down to the corner of the neighboring house and looked up at the window where the camera stood. Seeing it in the corner of the window, she wondered if anyone else had seen anything from this vantage point.

She turned her head and looked at the home next door but saw no signs of anyone about, and frankly, unsure if she should stir something up just yet, she decided to go back to the office and get some advice about how to handle this situation. Then she'd take a drive this evening after dark to see if there was anything going on in that room.

7

T he blonde looked down the street, then back inside the vehicle. Her eyes landed on his and he couldn't look away. Charly kept the conversation going.

"It's a nice neighborhood. Seems quiet and everyone's homes are nicely kept. We'd love to live here."

The blonde took a deep breath. "Houses seldom go up for sale here. I bought my house five years ago and I had to bid against several other buyers."

"Wow. That explains why there doesn't seem to be anything here."

"Yeah. My best advice is to make contact with a realtor and get on their call list for when something comes up. That's how I did it."

Charly nodded. "Thank you. My name is Charly. This is Van." She pointed to the blonde's house. "Is that your house?"

"Hi, my name is Hadleigh. Yes, that's my house."

"You do a great job keeping it neat and tidy."

Hadleigh looked at her lawn. "I don't do it alone. I have a kid that comes and mows the lawn each week. I work a lot of hours and don't always have time to get to it."

"Wow, what do you do?"

Her smile faded and she inhaled a deep breath before responding. "I'm a social worker. It's been a rough day."

"Oh, I'm sorry. I'm sure that's a tough job."

Hadleigh smiled and her eyes darted to him, likely wondering why he was sitting like a stone. The problem was, he was conflicted. She seemed sweet enough but he thought she could just be acting. She was doing something at that house with all of those kids. A social worker didn't come and go with all sorts of kids.

"It can be. It's also rewarding, too."

"Aww. That's nice to hear."

Hadleigh stepped back. "Well, good luck with finding a home in the neighborhood. Hopefully, I'll see you around soon."

"Thank you. Finger's crossed." Charly chuckled.

They watched Hadleigh turn and walk to her house, sorting through her mail as she walked.

Van put the SUV in gear and slowly drove down the street.

Charly sat back in her seat and stared straight ahead. After a few moments she said, "Well her job explains a lot."

"Does it? Like what?"

"Like what she's doing with the kids."

"Do social workers take kids out for walks? Bring other kids back?"

"Yes, I bet they do. Don't you think it makes sense that she'd want to chat with them out of ear shot of their foster parents to make sure the kids feel comfortable telling her what's going on?"

Van drove in silence for a while. Charly could be right, but he wasn't ready to give up his suspicions just yet. Hadleigh was still hiding something, he was sure of it.

His gut told him to drive back to the house on Station Street where he'd be meeting with Marco48 in a couple of days. Turning right, he navigated to the street.

Charly turned her head toward him. "Are we going back to the house?"

"Yeah. My gut doesn't sit right with this. Why would Marco48 want to meet with me and message me from a house that has a social worker visiting regularly? Isn't he getting kids being brought to his house on a regular basis? I don't understand anyone taking the risk."

"Van." Charly paused. "Why would anyone take the risk to meet people online without knowing they are who they say they are? We've gone over all this in training multiple times. They are sick in the head. They feel invincible.

They never believe they'll get caught and they love the thrill. Any or all of these things could be at play here."

"How could a social worker worth her salt not know something was going on?"

"How do you know she doesn't suspect something and is trying to figure it out?"

He let out a held breath in a whoosh and his shoulders deflated. "If that's the case, she'll screw up my investigation if she isn't careful or doesn't know what she's doing."

Charly turned to face forward and slumped back in the seat. "We've worked a long time to get this guy to trust us. That would suck and he could likely get away."

"Yeah."

Van turned onto Station Street from the opposite end of the street he'd driven down earlier today, now on the same side of the street as the house and slowed his speed. He didn't want to seem suspicious but he wanted to get a good look; he slowed a bit more. As they approached the house, the younger boy who'd run away earlier today was just now walking up the sidewalk.

"Look. He's back."

The younger boy looked to be of Hispanic descent, his clothing was clean, his hair combed and his shoes looked to be in good shape. This was not a street kid; he had someone who cared for him.

A man opened the door to him, looked down the street, then stepped back to let him in the house. The man seemed to be in his late twenties or early thirties. Brown hair which needed to be combed, sweat pants, and a t-shirt. He actually looked like he'd just gotten out of bed.

After the boy entered the home, the man stepped back inside and closed the door.

"What do you make of that?"

Charly watched the house closely but didn't say anything just yet. Then a light clicked on in the upstairs of the home and her eyes shifted to stare at the window.

"Can you see anything?" He couldn't from where he sat in the car. Since he only had adequate vision in his right eye, he needed to keep his eye on the road.

"No, the shade is pulled."

Looking at the clock Van said, "It's only six pm right now, I can't imagine anyone is going to bed just yet."

"Right." Charly looked up at the window again and saw shadows passing by the window. The curtain moved and something was pulled from behind the curtain, then the curtain fell in front of the window once again.

Hadleigh tried calling her boss and mentor, Lucy, once again. It'd been a couple of hours and still she hadn't been able to reach her. Her stomach had been twisted since she'd discovered the camera and Bethany's response to it. She wanted to march right back there and demand to know what was going on. But that wouldn't do her any good and might even hurt the children more.

Dialing Lucy's number once more, she listened as the phone rang but no one answered. She stopped pacing long enough to hear Lucy's message.

"Hi, this is Lucy, leave me a voicemail and I'll call you back."

"Hi Lucy, it's Hadleigh. I have a serious situation and need to run it by you. I'm simply not sure what to do and how to handle this."

Tapping the end call icon, Hadleigh grabbed her purse off the counter by the back door and walked out to the garage.

Maybe if she staked out the Connerts' house, she'd notice some activity in the storage room. As she drove, she ran all possible scenarios through her mind. Bethany's brother, Brent, could be taking pictures. She honestly hadn't looked like she knew what was going on when Hadleigh discovered the camera. Melvyn could be the photographer, which didn't seem right. Hadleigh tried remembering when she'd first come to the Connert home and had inspected it with Lucy. They'd looked over the house completely for their first placement. That was ten years ago, when Hadleigh was first starting out as a social worker. She'd been fresh from college and so excited to start in her new career. Still naive in thinking she was helping place needy children with good families to be taken care of until their parents could get their acts together. In all this time, she could count on one hand the parents and children who had been reunited. Bad parents, or addicted parents, seldom got their lives in order. She'd seen so many almost make a complete recovery only to relapse just when the pressure became too much and the possibility of getting their kids back came closer.

Melvyn, at that time, had been a fortyish year old man who worked for a car dealership in the finance department. He and Bethany had tried for years to have their own children and had been unsuccessful. Melvyn had been more reluctant to bring troubled kids into the home, but his wife meant the world to him and he easily went along with Bethany to make her happy. Over the years,

Hadleigh had been involved in or had placed more than thirty-three children with the Connerts.

Their home changed very little in all that time other than the fresh coat of paint and new living room furniture a few years ago. Bethany took great pride in her clean home and the children were always well fed and clothed. Bethany took great pains in teaching the kids how to take care of themselves, always concerned that when they aged out of the system and found themselves on their own that they'd struggle to know the basics of self-care. That's what made her such a great foster mom.

Turning up Station Street, Hadleigh stared up at the Connert home. The window of the room where the camera had been glowed; the light was on. Someone was in there. Were they removing the camera and backdrop or were they using it?

She parked behind another car on the street just a short distance from the Connerts' home. She got out, walked around to the sidewalk, then leaned on the side of her car and stared up at the lit window. Shadows floated by the window and she tried to determine who was up there.

"What are you doing here?" A male voice startled her. She swung her head around to face the man standing on the sidewalk in front of her.

"Excuse me?"

"I think you heard what I said, what are you doing here?"

It wasn't quite dark yet but she recognized him as the man in the car with the chatty blonde on her street this afternoon. Her heartbeat increased as her brain registered all sorts of warnings. She straightened up and stood tall, though he was still taller by several inches. "I could ask you the same question. Are you following me?"

"Hardly, since I was here first." He nodded to his car, parked just in front of hers, and she realized she'd pulled in behind him. Too much of a coincidence usually meant it wasn't.

She swallowed the lump in her throat and slowly reached into her back pocket for her cell phone only to realize she'd left it in the cup holder in her car.

"I just came back to look for something."

"Look for something or at something? Because it looks like you're staring up at that house."

She worked at keeping her voice steady, "What are you doing here?"

The blonde, his wife, came walking from the backyard then stopped and looked at her. "What are you doing here?"

"Your husband just asked me the same thing."

Charly shook her head, "Okay. So, he's not my husband."

Hadleigh looked into Van's eyes. His left eye appeared to not focus or engage her but his right eye was a beautiful blue. Almost like the summer sky blue.

"Your marital status isn't really my concern."

The door opened to the house and Hadleigh stepped to the side to see who was leaving. It was Brent and along with him was the young boy she'd seen here earlier today.

Brent stopped and looked at her, the expression on his face one of confusion before he turned and walked the other direction. The young boy walked toward them and Hadleigh stepped deeper into the sidewalk. "Hey, can I ask what you were doing inside the Connerts' home?"

He simply shook his head and kept walking. Now she could follow him. He clearly lived close by because he was walking. Wrestling with following him or going back to arguing with these two, it seemed the choice was clear. But she was intrigued as to what they were doing here and she wondered if they knew about something she didn't.

9

V an watched her. Hadleigh she'd said her name was. She stared after the young boy for some time then turned to face Charly and him.

"Look, I don't know what's going on in there, but something tells me it isn't good. I'm trying to figure it out."

Van glanced at Charly, then turned to Hadleigh. "Just let it go, please."

"I can't."

"Why not?" He counted as he exhaled, telling himself to stay calm. "Look, we can't say just yet what we're doing here, but suffice it to say it's important that nothing happen until we've been able to complete our task."

Hadleigh crossed her arms in front of her, total protective pose. "Well, I have a task to do as well and mine is to keep those kids safe. No one will stop me from doing that."

Van inhaled deeply, about ready to let this meddling woman have it when Charly stepped in.

"So, we all have the same goals. We need to accomplish them without harming anyone's chances of completing our tasks. How can we go about doing that?"

Hadleigh's eyes darted to his and he refused to look away. She was a beautiful woman and in this dusky light, with nothing but the orangish hues streaming through the trees, her hair looked like it was woven with golden threads. The color of her cheeks brightened as she worked to control her anger with him. Her jaw was set, her back rigid and he saw her fists ball up under her crossed arms. "Are you cops?"

Van, now calmer, responded, "No, we're not cops. Look, I can tell you that we're trained to ferret out pedophiles and traffickers and we're watching this house. It's imperative to our investigation that nothing interferes with this mission. We're close. So close."

"If you aren't cops, who are you? There aren't any private agencies that do this kind of work. I'd know about them in my line of work."

Charly answered her first. "We're hired by the government sometimes. By grieving parents of lost children some-times. By local authorities sometimes. We're private because we can move the lines of propriety when we need to where law enforcement can't. But mostly, we take our job very seriously. We should be allies in this. We have the same goals."

"So then, why were you at my house?" she challenged.

He ignored Charly's glance and studied Hadleigh's eyes. They were a beautiful shade of brown, framed in thick lashes. He could see the fine lines at the corners of her eyes and guessed her age in her early thirties.

"We were checking you out. We weren't sure if you were part of the problem and were doing our jobs. Which, by the way, we are very good at."

Hadleigh bit her bottom lip. His heartbeat kicked up a notch and he got mad at himself for the involuntary reaction of his body. He didn't want to think she was sexy; she was stubborn and frustrating. Stupid feelings.

Hadleigh looked up at the window again, before turning her pretty face to his. "Should we go somewhere and share what we know?"

Charly responded immediately. "That's a great idea. Why don't we get out of here before they see us and suspect something?"

Charly nudged Van and he reluctantly nodded agreement. "Let's go to the Copper Cup and have a drink and talk."

He watched Hadleigh swallow a lump in her throat, he had one too, but at this point they might as well try and work together. Somewhat.

Van jumped into the driver's seat and started the SUV as Charly climbed inside. He pulled from the curb as soon as Charly closed her door and gathered his thoughts on all of this. Things were moving fast and he felt like he was drowning trying to keep up.

"It's all good Van. She has some information and so do we. If we combine what we all know we have a better chance of stopping this guy."

He exhaled. "What exactly are our restrictions on working with anyone else? For this job, we're hired by the Bureau but I haven't had a minute to see if that means we have to stay under the radar or if we can work with other agencies. Hadleigh is a social worker, that means she works for the county, maybe the state. We need to have those questions answered first."

"Right. Let me log onto the system and see if we have parameters. I'll also send Emmy a text just to be sure."

Charly's fingers, at least the fingers on her right hand, were flying over the keyboard as fast as she could do it. Which, to Van's amazement, was about as fast as he could type with two hands.

Pulling in at the back of the Copper Cup, he noted the parking lot was only partially full, which was good; they'd have a bit of privacy to chat.

"I'll bring my laptop inside and keep working while we chat."

Taking a deep breath Van nodded, "Okay, we'll start with getting her information and go from there."

Charly closed the lid on her laptop, tucked it into her computer bag, and opened her door. Van locked the doors as they walked into the Copper Cup.

He held the door for Charly. Despite her clicking tongue, he would always be a gentleman, didn't matter that the women he worked with thought of themselves as one of the gang. They were, and important parts at that, but he was raised properly and he'd always do what was right. He'd argue the point to anyone who complained. His mother and father would be proud to know that despite his tattoos and military experience, he'd remained a gentleman.

Charly found an empty table while he looked around for Hadleigh.

A waitress came over to them. "What'll you folks have?"

Charly answered first. "I'll have an iced tea with no sugar. Van, what are you having?"

Van looked at the waitress; he hadn't seen her before. Red hair, a sparkly piercing in her nose and bright blue eyes. "I'll have a root beer."

"That it for you folks?"

"No, we're waiting for someone to meet us." He absently stated.

He didn't see Hadleigh anywhere and had to admit to himself that he wasn't paying attention when he drove over here. She should have been right behind them. That woman had his head in a spin for sure and he needed to get it on straight. Their future missions could be in jeopardy if he didn't. They wanted that five-year contract with the Bureau and he wanted Marco48 off the streets before he harmed any other children. Then he wanted the rest of those assholes to go down for the harm they did to kids. All of them, and he'd work till his dying day to do it, too.

The door opened and he looked up. Disappointment flooded his body when a man in his fifties walked in and not Hadleigh. Where in the hell was she?

10

H adleigh pulled over to the side of the street a few doors down from the Copper Cup at the Main Street entrance. She'd followed Van and Charly until they turned off to go around back, but she preferred the front entrance. Gathering her purse and checking herself in the mirror on her visor, she added a bit of lip gloss and pronounced herself good. After all, she wasn't trying to impress him. Them. Anyone. This was just an information-gathering conversation and that would be it.

Checking her mirror one more time, she swiped under her left eye with the pad of her ring finger and blinked. That was better. It still didn't matter though.

Hadleigh stepped from her car as a brand-new white Cadillac Escalade pulled to the curb across the street. It caught her attention because her brother had recently chatted about a friend of his purchasing one. In Holden's words, "They're hella expensive."

The gleaming white vehicle looked odd on the streets of Lynyrd Station. This town was small, and while not poor at all, it didn't regularly have expensive sports cars or high-end luxury vehicles such as this.

Hadleigh did a double take when the door to the escalade opened. The middle-aged man who stepped out was a dead ringer for Melvyn Connert. As he walked across the street to the Copper Cup her jaw practically dropped open. It was Melvyn all right, and how in the hell could he afford a brand-new Escalade?

She watched him open the door to the restaurant, his chest puffed out, face gleaming with pride. Thinking back to the last time she'd paid attention to the Connerts' vehicles, a sick dread filled her stomach. She hadn't. Not in a long time. In her defense, she had no reason to pay attention to that. Every visit she'd made had seemed as though things were perfectly fine. Until today.

Pulling her phone from her purse, she tapped the phone number of Lucy Carlisle once more to see if she could get her on the phone. She really wanted some guidance on this.

She listened as the phone rang and rang, with a heavy sigh, she ended the call and dropped her phone into her purse. She walked to the door of the Copper Cup and opened it.

The delicious aroma of the food this place served surrounded her and her stomach growled in anger as she hadn't fed it anything since lunch today. She lay her hand over her irritated tummy and looked around for Charly and Van.

Van stood then and waved to her from the table at the back of the room. She waved back, which was silly but she did, and walked toward them. She ignored the suddenly-active butterflies in her tummy. Mostly because it was stupid to get excited by him. She didn't even know what his relationship with Charly was. Earlier Charly said they were married, then she said they weren't.

As she reached the table, Van stood and held her chair out and her stupid cheeks flushed. "Thank you."

She sat at Van's right and directly across from Charly. It was then that she noticed Charly's left hand and arm from the elbow down was a prosthetic.

Charly smiled. "I was shot while in the service. It had to be amputated. The only thing it inhibits is my ability to type fast."

Van laughed. "You still type faster than I do."

Charly smiled brightly. "You suck at typing. Period."

He smiled at Charly and Hadleigh realized just how handsome he was. His whiskers were dark blonde to match his hair, but it gave him a rugged look, which was belied by his hair; which was almost shaved at the sides, the top left longer but combed back. That told her he cared about his appearance. But the gray t-shirt he wore showed his arms, which were both covered in tattoos. This again made him look badass. To be honest, she wondered at his layers. Was he like an onion? How many layers would she have to pull back to find out who he really was?

Charly looked across the table at her, "So, we ordered drinks and I see the waitress bringing them now. What do you want—I'm buying."

"You don't have to buy me anything."

Charly laughed. "I know, I want to. I'm going to have a piece of pie. Have you had their cherry pie here? It's like a slice of heaven."

The waitress brought the previously ordered drinks. "Did I hear you wanted pie?"

Charly's eyes danced. "Yes, cherry with whipped cream on top."

She wrote it down and looked her way. "I'd like a piece of cherry pie with whipped cream as well. And a..." She glanced at Van's drink and it was a frosted mug of root beer. "Is that root beer? I'd love one of those."

"You got it."

She looked at Van who only shook his head, "Nothing else for me thank you."

The waitress turned and walked away and Hadleigh's eyes landed on Melvyn Connert, who sat at the bar with a couple of male friends laughing.

She inhaled deeply and let it out slowly then turned to see Charly and Van watching her.

Her cheeks heated at their stares and she delicately cleared her throat. "Melvyn Connert walked in just before me. He's sitting at the bar. The man with the white button up shirt. He got out of a new Escalade."

Van's eyes looked in the direction she'd pointed out and watched the men at the bar.

"You mentioned the Connert home to the little boy that left the house we were standing in front of. The only owner of record we could find on that house was an LLC."

"Yes, Mrs. Connert has an LLC. It was inherited from her family and she became the registered agent upon her father's death. They bought the house under the LLC to keep assets in it."

"Before that, two other LLCs owned that same house."

Hadleigh shrugged. "I don't know anything about the previous owners."

"Okay. So Mr. Connert, Melvyn, has a brand-new Cadillac and that's not something they can afford?"

Hadleigh looked into Van's eyes, so blue, except his left eye, which had some clouding in it.

"Mr. Connert is a finance coordinator at a car dealership. He helps people obtain financing to buy cars. He makes okay money but not enough to be able to afford an Escalade. Even if he got a hefty discount from the dealership, still it would be way out of his price range. Mrs. Connert doesn't work outside the home and the only other income for them is the money they get from having foster children, which is less than $1,000 per month. From that the kids have to be fed and clothed, plus any school activities the foster parents let them participate in. The Connerts have always been very generous to their foster children and treated them as their own."

Van watched Melvyn Connert. "So where did this money come from then?"

11

As Van watched Melvyn Connert chat with his friends at the bar, he noticed that Melvyn excused himself to use the restroom. Van decided it was a great time to use it himself.

"I'm going to the restroom." He told Charly and Hadleigh but his eyes never left Melvyn.

Hadleigh's shoulders pulled back and she sat straighter. Charly nodded, but said nothing. As he walked to the back of the bar, he ran through his mind the things that were said during his chat messages with Marco48. He had said Van could make money if he wanted too. Immediately Van was irritated with him but kept his cool.

Van: "Oh really? I need money."

Marco48: "Oh yes, there is much to be made. Send me a picture of you so I can tell you how much you can make."

Van had Caiden Marx from their Cyber team create a profile and several pictures for him to share. They weren't real photos, just images he cut and pasted together to create a human profile for Van to use.

Sending one of the pictures, Van replied, "I have this one. Does this work?"

Marco48: "Very much. You can make a lot of money. Do you have one with your shirt off?"

Swallowing the vomit in his throat Van turned to Caiden. "Fucker wants one with my shirt off."

Caiden's lip curled in disgust but he played on his computer and created a picture with no shirt on.

"Just sent it over to you." Caiden growled. "You've got to get this piece of shit."

"I intend to."

Van clicked open the photo and saved it to his computer, then sent it on to Marco48. "I only have this one right now. I'll have to have someone help me take more."

Marco48: "That won't be necessary, I can help with that."

Van: "Thank you. I'm excited to make money."

Marco48: "I'll be in touch soon."

They ended that chat and Van assumed Marco48 went to beat off to the bare chest of a young boy. He went up to his apartment and took a shower. It made him feel dirty dealing with these pedos.

This would be his first time seeing Marco48 face to face and he vacillated between being disgusted and being excited to finally be one step closer to nailing the son-of-a-bitch.

He entered the bathroom just as the door was swinging closed from Marco48 entering. He saw the middle-aged man standing in front of a mirror but looking at his phone. Van tried to see what was on his screen but he couldn't see anything because Melvyn quickly pocketed his phone. His cheeks tinted pink but all he did was nod at Van and turn toward the wall of stalls and disappear.

Van turned on the water and washed his hands, then splashed his face. Pulling a couple of towels from the white metal holder on the wall he patted his face dry then tossed the toweling.

Leaning on the sink he waited until he heard Melvyn flush the toilet and unlock the door. Van once again turned the water on and began washing his hands. Melvyn walked to the sink next to Van's and began washing his hands. Van looked into the mirror and caught Melvyn's gaze.

"I haven't seen you in here much."

Melvyn shook his head. "No, I used to go to the Hotshot, but that closed. So my friends and I have been meeting here a couple nights a week for a few beers."

"Oh, yeah, I heard Hotshot had closed."

"Yeah. It wasn't the nicest bar in town and they got caught up in drugs and distribution so... that's what they get I guess."

"Yep, that'll do it." Van looked at him in the mirror again. "Did I see you get out of that new Caddy out front?"

Melvyn's mouth parted in the biggest smile he'd ever seen. "Yep, just got her last night. My wife has been saving up and she did good."

Van whistled. "I'll say. That's a good wife you have there."

"She's the best."

"What does a vehicle like that go for these days?"

"I get a discount from work, but they run between $76,000 on up to close to $90,000 depending on options."

Van whistled again. "I can't even imagine what that monthly payment would be. I'm still trying to buy a house."

Van pulled a couple sheets of toweling from the wall and dried his hands. Melvyn did the same.

Melvyn pulled a business card from his wallet. "I work at Top End Automotive as the finance coordinator. Maybe I can help you get into a vehicle you'd enjoy. Though, the payments on this one will run you about $1,800 a month unless you have a serious down-payment."

"Whoa, that's way too steep for me. Maybe I need to get a job where you work."

Melvyn laughed. "Not a bad idea, but if it weren't for my wife, I wouldn't have it either. She paid cash for it from the money she saved. Nice chatting."

Melvyn nodded and exited the bathroom while Van gave him a minute before leaving. He came off as a nice man, just a good ole boy and humble. His online persona was different, more direct and to the point. But then again, behind the keyboard even the meekest mouse can turn into a rat.

Van walked back to his table and sat down. "I didn't get much. He works at Top End Automotive and bought the Caddy from there. Said his wife saved up to buy it for him, she paid cash. Used to hang out at Hotshot till it closed. Has beers with his buddies a couple times a week."

Charly sucked in some air. "Cash? That costs what...?"

"About $80 grand I'm thinking."

Charly coughed.

Hadleigh tucked her long blonde hair behind her left ear as she studied the table. "I think I might be able to check into some of the financials. I have access from the office. I'll check on his income and what their mortgage payment is. I still don't see how she could have saved enough to buy this vehicle.

Charly leaned forward and across the table. "What else can you tell us about the home Hadleigh?"

Hadleigh stared at Charly for a brief moment then she licked her lips. He liked that. He didn't want to, but she was magnetic in some way.

"I thought this was the perfect foster family. I've placed dozens of kids with them. The kids never complain, their clothes are always clean, they always have food, and the Connerts are always generous in allowing the kids things like after-school sports and concerts or other extracurriculars."

Van stared at Hadleigh and she turned to look directly into his eyes. "What changed?"

Hadleigh swallowed and bit her bottom lip again. He wished she'd stop doing that. "I saw a camera today. It was behind a curtain in that upstairs room."

"Why does that bother you?" He kept his voice even.

"Because it was hidden. Because Autumn was wearing lip stick and she's only eight. Because there's now a male living in the home, if even for only a few weeks, and Autumn seems to like him. His bedroom is directly across the hall from hers. I'm always wary when a child begins to exhibit more mature behaviors."

"What did you do about it?"

Hadleigh took a deep breath and let it out in a whoosh. "I tried calling my boss, but I haven't gotten her on the phone. I don't have any evidence. I'd hate to accuse the Connerts of something if they aren't guilty. They're good...they have been good foster parents to so many kids."

"So you don't want to write up a report because you might lose a foster family?"

Hadleigh's eyes rounded and her mouth dropped open. "I didn't say that! I didn't mean that. Not at all."

Van crossed his arms across his chest as he stared at Hadleigh. The stare down had begun.

12

D id he just accuse her of not caring about the kids at all? He did. That just steamed her up good. She opened her mouth to say something, but words wouldn't come out.

She crossed her arms over her chest and stared at his insolent, stupid, handsome face. She opened her mouth again to let him have it when Charly stepped in.

"So, let's not make this nasty." She turned and looked at Van, "You didn't mean that Hadleigh didn't care for the kids, did you Van?"

He inhaled deeply and let it out slowly. "No, I didn't exactly mean that. But, isn't it her job to write up a report when she suspects something going on?"

Charly turned to look at her and merely raised her eyebrows.

"Yes, well sort of. I only found a camera and nothing else. No pictures. A camera is not a weapon. It's not illegal. It isn't proof of anything going on that shouldn't be going on. The Connerts do not have a history of taking child pornography pictures. It could very well be someone taking pictures of items to sell on the internet in that room. So, I wanted to check with my boss to see what her take is on this."

Charly smiled at her and she felt a bit at ease. "You're right. And, Van..." Charly looked at Van and he her, "If Hadleigh had gone off and written a report without knowing all the facts, it could have alerted them to the fact that they're being watched. So, in this instance at least, we should be very happy that she didn't file a report yet."

Hadleigh watched as Van exhaled and relaxed. "Right." His tone was clipped and Hadleigh got the distinct impression that he just wanted a reason to be mad at her. Jerk.

The waitress brought their pies and oh man, did they look great. "Here you go folks. Anything else I can get for you?"

She stared at her pie, wondering how she'd eat it all and Charly replied to the waitress. "Nope, that's it for now."

All Hadleigh could do was nod.

Charly took a big bite of her pie; whipped cream smooshed on her top lip but she didn't care. A loud, "Mmm," came from Charly and Hadleigh dove into her pie.

Charly swallowed and said, "So, Hadleigh, you can look into their finances and see what some of their banking looks like. Whether Melvyn has gotten a raise or raises and bonuses and let us know?"

"I can look into it, yes. As to sharing the information, I'll need to check."

Charly's nose wrinkled at that but Hadleigh took that moment to fork another large bit of pie into her mouth. As she chewed, she had to work to keep her eyes from rolling into the back of her head. The pie was truly a slice of heaven. Of course, she was famished, so there was that.

She glanced at Van, who was staring at her. She stopped chewing for a moment, licked her lips and tasted the whipped cream on them. And realized she probably looked like she'd plunged face-first into the dessert.

Van stared for a few moments then blinked and shook his head. "That's all well and good, but he told me his wife had saved for the vehicle. That doesn't mean the banking would show us much unless she manages the money in the house, including where his checks are spent."

Hadleigh swallowed her mouthful of pie and licked her lips again. "As I recall, Bethany does manage the money. Melvyn is a fairly hands-off guy. He's quiet, reserved, and sort of low-key."

Van nodded and Hadleigh cut off another piece of her pie with her fork. Scooping it up, she hesitated to make sure they weren't going to ask her a question, before she took her bite.

Charly set her fork down, picked up her drink and wet her throat. "So, let's talk about the brother. Who is he and where is he from?"

Hadleigh swallowed her pie. "All I know is he's a location scout for a movie studio and he's visiting here for three weeks or so. I suppose the camera could be his, it would seem that a location scout would have cameras to send pictures back to the studio before securing a place. His name is Brent Jennings. He's handsome, in his forties, in good shape. Looks like a Hollywood type."

"Well, as long as he's handsome, that's all that matters." Van snapped.

Hadleigh raised her eyebrows at the same time she straightened her shoulders.

Charly laughed. "You asked about the brother, Hadleigh told you what she knows."

Van inhaled deeply and slowly let it out. Hadleigh watched his chest rise and fall and her cheeks heated. Again. His chest looked impressive. Firm and broad and built. He likely worked out. Which. Did. Not. Matter. Maybe she'd been without a boyfriend for too long; even she saw a pattern developing in her train of thought today.

"I did ask. Sorry," he responded.

Charly then swallowed and offered some relief. "Was that Brent who left the house when we were there? He went in the opposite direction as the young boy."

"Yes, that was him."

Van then pulled his phone off the table and began sending a text. She couldn't see what he was typing or to whom, and she didn't want to get caught staring so she took another bite of pie while there was time.

As she and Charly neared the end of their pie, Hadleigh took a moment to ask her own questions. "What do you know about the Connerts? Why were you there tonight?"

Van set his phone on the table and looked at her. "We have reason to suspect there is something going on in that house that isn't on the legal side of things and that it involves children."

"What information do you have?"

"We can't say at this point. All I can say is someone in that house is involved in pornography."

"Who?"

13

He wasn't ready or interested in telling her everything. And, for God's sake, he wished she'd stop licking her lips. Every time her tongue darted out between her lips and swiped along their fullness, he got edgy. He should have had Charly sitting at his right, that way Hadleigh would have sat to his left and he wouldn't be able to see her that well out of his bad eye.

"Who was the young boy who left the house after you arrived?" He needed to get what they could get from her then get the hell out of here.

"I don't know. I saw him this afternoon and as soon as he saw me, he took off. Autumn wouldn't say anything when I asked her. She just shrugged."

"And you didn't press her for more information?"

"No, I didn't. To be honest, at the time it didn't mean anything to me and didn't have any bearing on anything going on in that house."

"How do you know he isn't one of the victims of the pornographer?"

"Until tonight, I didn't know anything about a pornographer. *AND*, if you know so much about a pornographer being in the house, what are you doing about it?"

He felt his body heat at her tone. She was getting angry with him and frankly, he was angry with her. Though he didn't know why.

Charly set her fork down and lay her right hand across her tummy. "Ugh, I'm stuffed now. But so happy."

He glanced her way and took a deep breath. He knew what she was doing, he simply wasn't in the mood to lighten the vibe right now. To be honest, he was downright irritated and he didn't even know exactly why. He just hoped by getting Hadleigh riled up she'd spill some good information.

Hadleigh looked at him then she delicately sniffed. "Are there sites where you can search to see if there are household items being sold on the internet from that location? What if Bethany is buying things at auctions and garage sales and selling them online?"

"How much stuff do you think you'd have to sell to raise about $80,000?"

"A lot, I guess." Her voice softened.

"Did you happen to see a bunch of stuff sitting around and did Bethany say anything about selling stuff?"

Hadleigh's shoulders slumped forward and she looked completely dejected. "No."

Van leaned forward and he softened his voice as well. "Would it make a difference, as to whether she could still keep the kids, if she sold things online?"

"No. Although if we thought the safety of the children was at risk, it would be cause for concern. But many people just do porch pickup for items and receive payment online."

"What did Bethany say when you saw the camera?"

Hadleigh bit her bottom lip and Van sat back in his chair and watched her. She was a beautiful, smart woman and he didn't like that he felt that way one bit.

"She seemed surprised. Said she didn't know whose it was."

Charly pushed her plate toward her left, to the edge of the table in front of the empty seat. "Hadleigh, have you ever known Bethany to fib a little? Would she lie about the camera because she was afraid having it and buying and selling things online was wrong?"

Hadleigh sat back in her chair, pulled her napkin from her lap and folded it neatly before setting it on the table next to her empty plate. "I've never felt she was a liar. Before she was my responsibility my boss placed many children with Bethany and Melvyn. All these years they never tried to adopt any of the kids but they always took care of them. They have never refused a child we needed to place, if even for only a few days. She's never seemed rattled or as if we were about to uncover anything. We've always been able to count on her."

"And in all that time, before you were responsible for them and after, what about Melvyn?"

Hadleigh's eyes darted to Melvyn across the restaurant, still sitting at the bar with his friends. Her head cocked to the left slightly as she stared. "You know, I almost never deal with Melvyn. It's always Bethany. When I've had to pick up children at night and Melvyn's been home, he just stays in his room or the living room watching television. He doesn't talk that much. He'll hold a crying child. I've seen him feed the babies and help out. But, when it comes to talking to him at length, I've never had that much to converse with him about. Bethany did all the talking and Melvyn just listened or nodded."

Slowly her head turned to him and when their eyes locked, she straightened and he saw her cheeks turn the prettiest shade of pink. He had a hard time looking away from her. He noticed the brown of her eyes was more akin to a deep brown with lighter streaks of brown in them. Interesting.

Thankfully, Charly broke the spell he was in. "So, Bethany is really the person who runs everything where the kids and the finances are concerned. Did she inherit money from her father when he passed away? You said she inherited the LLC but did that LLC hold other assets that Bethany inherited? Does she have more than the one brother?"

Hadleigh smiled at Charly and he saw a hint of a dimple. "It's just Bethany and Brent. I'd never met him before today. I admit I was surprised he was there. As to an inheritance, I don't believe there was anything of any real value that she inherited. I can check though."

"Would you and let us know? We'd love to be able to find out who from that address is harming children and stop them. But, like you, we don't want to accuse anyone who is innocent and harm a perfectly good reputation."

"Yes, I'll let you know. But what are you going to do from this point?"

He leaned forward, setting his arms on the table, and watched as her eyes roamed over the tattoos he loved so much. They were wing dings and ding bats of fonts of the brothers and sisters in the military that he'd lost. He had a tattoo artist that brought them together beautifully and he'd readily admit that every time he had to make another appointment, his stomach knotted up once again for the purpose.

"I have a meeting set up with Marco48 later this week. While you're doing your research, we'll do ours."

Her beautiful brown eyes snapped to his when he spoke and he stared into them. Deep. Something just happened as he continued to hold the contact with her. It was as if they were trying to figure each other out. Hers were shiny and bright and intelligent. They darted back and forth between his eyes and he knew she could see the difference in his. It made him feel as though he should explain away his deficiency and his stomach tightened at the thought that Hadleigh would think less of him.

"How will you meet with him if you're a grown man and he's into kids?"

"I'm going to show up and talk to him. My colleagues will be with me..." He motioned to Charly, "Then we'll get what we can from him while we wait for the police to come in and arrest him."

"When are you meeting him?" Her voice was soft and they continued to stare at each other.

"Thursday."

14

H adleigh sat in her car and ran her conversation with Donovan and Charly through her mind. They'd never mentioned the name of their organization, which, shame on her, she should have insisted on. They genuinely seemed to want to help children, which had always been her goal since she was a little girl, and the horrible things her cousin Hannah and her Aunt Marnie endured had left their imprint on her forever.

She turned her head and looked at the Escalade still sitting across the street and knew she had some work to do. Turning the key in the ignition, she started her drive home. She'd likely not sleep much tonight; her brain was still buzzing with so many things.

As she walked into her house, Hadleigh set her purse on the counter and walked directly to her office. Opening the lid on her laptop, she logged into her computer at work and pulled down the list of sites they'd compiled where children were easily targeted. She had to swallow the disgust that filled her as she typed in the address bar to one of them.

Immediately her screen filled with pictures of kids in adult poses and skimpy clothing. Her stomach twisted as she averted her eyes toward the search bar and typed in Marco48, the man Van was meeting with and whom he suspected was Melvyn Connert.

His name popped up but since she didn't have a profile for the site, she had to create one to touch base with him.

Taking a deep breath and looking over some of the other profiles she reminded herself to speak as if she were immature and noticed most of them used the common internet acronyms like lol, and lmfao, fwiw. She so hated those acronyms, kids forgot how to actually spell because of stuff like this. The dumbing down of America, actually the world, right there.

So, she wrote a brief profile, said she was a foster kid and hated where she lived and wanted to make some money to get out of her situation. Then it came time for a picture and she once again swallowed her queasy feelings of being unclean and searched through her pictures on her computer. She had some from a "Throwback Thursday" post she'd done a while ago, so she looked through those.

Coming up on a photograph of her and her cousin, Hannah, in the little blow-up swimming pool in their backyard when they were around nine years old. There she and Hannah stood, their arms around each other in their little bikinis, their opposite arms on their hips. Her mom had laughed so hard when this picture had been developed. "You two look so cute Hadleigh. I'm going to get a couple of copies of this for Hannah and one for you too. This is priceless."

Gawd, she missed her mom as much as she missed Hannah. They were inseparable for so many years. Until Hannah and Aunt Marnie died. Then three years later Hadleigh's mom died too. Life had propelled her on a journey then, her journey to save the world of lonely, abused, sad, children. She'd done a pretty good job of it until recently. She used the name HanMarn as her profile name since no one used their real names and waited as the little circle twirled on her computer, letting her know it was working.

Her phone rang and she picked it up from her desk, excited when she saw Lucy's name on the screen.

"Hi Lucy, I'm so happy to hear from you."

"I got all your messages Hadleigh and I'm sorry I wasn't able to return your call sooner. I'm here at the hospital with my mom, she had a stroke, and I have to keep my phone off when I'm in her room."

"Oh, Lucy, I'm so sorry to hear about your mom. What is her prognosis?"

"It's not good Hadleigh. She's in her upper nineties now, and she'll likely not pull through this one. It's the third stroke she's had this year and this one was a bad one."

"Oh, Lucy." She stopped to get her voice under control. She took a deep breath, "If there is anything I can do, please let me know."

"Thank you. You just keep doing a good job and keep things under control at the office and we'll be fine."

That comment had her heart thumping and she didn't want to dump any of this on Lucy right now. But Lucy, being herself and likely needing something else to think about, asked, "What are your suspicions about the Connerts?"

Quickly telling Lucy of the lipstick and the camera and now the Escalade, she waited for Lucy's response.

"Well, Hadleigh, all these things together do add up, and not for the good of the children, but you don't really have anything to go on to make a complaint. A little girl playing dress-up, a camera in an unused room, and a new car; no matter how expensive, aren't reason for a write up."

Hadleigh let out her breath and felt oddly relieved and also frustrated because Van and Charly thought there was something going on. But she hadn't told Lucy about them, which now struck her as odd.

"But, that being said, you can check into things privately without alerting the higher-ups until there is further proof."

"But..."

"Yes, I know, in the meantime something might be happening in that home that we should be taking care of, but we don't have that information now. Get it as quickly as you can, and we can pull the children from the home. You can check the bank records, look for deposits outside of Melvyn's payday and our payment to them for child-care. You can check the file to find their mortgage company and you can check credit card statements. Then, you can also do a follow-up employment verification on

Melvyn, we have all the authorizations in the file. You should be able to check all of that tomorrow."

"Thank you, Lucy. I appreciate the guidance. I knew all of these things but wasn't sure about this one as it seems a bit out of the norm."

"We're always looking for out of the norm, Hadleigh. Call me and leave a message anytime. I'll get back to you when I can."

"Thank you. Try and take care of yourself too, Lucy."

"Yes. Right." The line went dead and Hadleigh smiled at the phone.

15

D onovan and Charly walked into the conference room. Normally a hive of activity, tonight it was only Emmy on her computer and Caiden Marx.

"Caiden, you're just the hacker I need to speak with." Van said as he walked to Caiden's computers.

"I'm not a hacker."

"Okay, man with the wicked hacker skills."

"Okay, so why are you flattering me?"

Charly chuckled and Van shook his head.

"I need some intel on Melvyn Connert. I also need some intel on Melvyn's brother-in-law, Brent Jennings."

Van gave Caiden the information he had currently and hoped that he'd be able to come up with more than that.

A quick glance at Emmy told him something was wrong. Her beautiful face was contorted as her brows were pulled tightly together and she bit the inside of her cheek.

He walked to her desk and she never looked up. "Hey, you okay?"

Her eyes snapped up and she started slightly as if she hadn't even noticed that he'd entered the room.

"Hey." She exhaled and sat back in her chair. "Yes and no."

"Anything you want to talk about?"

The air left her lungs in a whoosh and she swallowed. "Remember the three kids we rescued the day we quit Operation Live Again? James, Olive, and Damien?"

Van nodded. "Of course, I'll never forget those kids and what they were almost left to."

Emmy rubbed her right temple with the tips of her right fingers. "It appears that Olive Tomms also has a sister. Haylie Tomms was kidnapped at the same time as Olive. Clearly they'd been separated but Haylie hasn't been recovered."

"Fuck."

"Yeah."

"How did you find this out?"

Emmy stood and froze as he'd seen her do so many times before. Her hip was a constant source of pain.

"Creed and I have been working to figure out who Sergeant Dildo's accomplices are. Doing a search through the kids to see who had them and where they'd been before we found them, I saw a police report. Trouble is, according to the police, they aren't actively searching for her anymore. They had to send it to the cold case room because the trail ran cold."

"Where are their fucking parents? Why aren't they livid about this?"

"Mom's a drunk. Dad comes and goes."

"I just hate that people have kids who have no business having kids. They can't or won't take care of them and it sickens my stomach."

"Mine too."

"Can I help?" His stomach flipped and he felt a bit nauseous but still would stay and help Emmy if he could.

"Not right now. I'm not sure which direction to turn on this one, but I'm going to sleep on it and come back at it in the morning. Thanks Van."

"Of course."

He turned and walked to Caiden once again and watched the man work those computers. He really was amazing at this stuff.

Charly sat at her desk across the room and Emmy limped over to chat with her.

Van looked at Caiden, "You good if I get some shut-eye?"

"Of course. I'll pull what I can together and have it on your desk in the morning."

"Thanks Caiden."

Van swiveled his head on his way out. The tightness in his shoulders and neck had been squeezing him for a few hours now, but it began to really pinch after they left the Copper Cup.

What was it about Hadleigh that got under his skin? Charly had told him on the ride home that she was trying to do a good thing. She was trying to make sure the kids in the house were being taken care of; not being taken advantage of.

He walked into his apartment, inhaled a deep breath and let it out slowly. He walked to the bedroom and tossed his wallet, watch, gun, and holster into the top drawer of his nightstand then made a bee-line for the shower.

As the warm water rolled over his body, he tried clearing his mind of everything so he could bring himself back to a center of peace. His vision had grown dimmer the more the muscles pinched in his neck and his head had begun to pound the more he tried to ignore it.

Van dried himself off, stepped into a pair of gray sweat-pants, and flopped on his bed. He stared at the ceiling for some time, regulated his breathing and relaxed. Tried to relax. Soon he'd relax.

Hadleigh walked to him and stretched her arms around his shoulders. The feel of her body against his was like warm sunshine touching bare skin. She felt warm and she fit him like a glove. Her hair smelled like summer flowers as they heated in the sun, their perfume floating in the air and wrapping anyone within reach in their aroma. He pulled her closer to him, the feeling of not being able to hold her tight enough filling him with frustration and urgency at the same time. Her lips kissed the shell of his ear, then along his jaw, under his ear to his neck, then behind his ear; his heart hammered in his chest. He felt soothed and relaxed and incredibly at ease with Hadleigh in his arms. Holding Hadleigh was clearly the balm to his wounds and the realization of that gave him the same happiness he felt when he uncovered a key piece of evidence to clear a case. Quite frankly, life was pretty fucking great when he was with Hadleigh. That's what he finally understood.

A loud bang made him jump, his eyes flew open, his breathing ragged and the pillow he had his arms wrapped around and smashed to his chest was now beginning to regain its shape. He blinked to wet his eyes and clear his head. He pushed himself upright, looked around his room and let out a breath. Then he realized that it was a dream. He shook his head, scrubbed his hands down his face, then twisted his body to let his legs fall to the floor. He had no business dreaming about Hadleigh Watterson. He really didn't even like her. That much. Perhaps a little bit, but...

16

Hadleigh's computer chimed the incoming message and she set the hot water pot on the burner. Bringing her cup with her, she sipped gingerly on the scorching hot tea as she walked to her office.

As soon as she opened the email, emotions ran through her. Many emotions. As in, excitement, repulsion, pride, irritation, and finally disgust.

Marco48 had responded to her inquiry about making money.

Marco48: "Hey there, it looks like you need to make some quick cash."

Hadleigh clicked reply and started typing. "Yes and quick. I need to get out of here fast. Foster father is handsy."

Marco48: "That's not good. Tell me what you're willing to do for money."

Her tea threatened to come up and she had to turn from her desk and breathe deep. So disgusting.

Remembering that doing this was to help all those kids who needed good people on their side, Hadleigh twisted her chair around and typed a reply.

"I'll do whatevs."

She saw the three dots jumping and knew he was typing out a response to her. Chancing a sip of her tea, she thought she'd likely need something else in her stomach if much more of this took place, so she quickly walked back to the kitchen and opened the cupboard above the coffee pot where she kept her emergency cookies. This was deemed an emergency in her mind. Pulling two chocolate cookies with cream filling from the package, she snagged a napkin from the holder on the counter then scooted back to her office to wait for Marco48's reply. She didn't have to wait long.

Marco48: "Whatevs leaves things a bit open. You can make a lot of money if you are willing to take your shirt off. A lot more if you're willing to pose nude."

The frown that formed on her face was so pronounced she could feel it. This guy was a fucking pig. No doubt. Little girls didn't have chests. What in the hell did grown-ass men like about that? It had to be a power thing. Dominance and control over someone and young girls didn't know any better so they put up with it. A young poor girl would do things she didn't want to, just to not be poor.

Hadleigh swallowed and inhaled a deep breath. Then she let it out slowly, took a calming sip of her tea and replied to Marco48."I'm willing to pose nude. How much is 'a lot more'?"

She waited for a while and no response came back to her. She stared out the window for quite some time, watched a few birds fight over something in the tree, likely a fat worm, which seemed more tasteful right now than what she was doing.

A few minutes later still nothing from Marco48 so Hadleigh took her empty cup to the kitchen, refilled it, and walked to her bathroom to begin her day in earnest.

After dressing in khakis and a light blue sweater for the day, Hadleigh let her hair fall over her shoulders to dry, then walked to her computer to see what Marco48's response had been.

It had been—no response. This surprised her but then again, it could be his tactic to make her really want to make money. She decided not to sit by the computer, and besides, she had work to do. Today was another day of home visits and appointments. Plus, she wanted to find some time to access the banking information for the Connerts and see what she could find out.

She was happy to see she was the first to arrive. That meant she'd have some time to do some research and look through the files. Deciding to start a spreadsheet on the Connerts and the finances they reported, she pulled their file from their central filing shelves then hurried to her desk which was in a small cramped room with another social worker, Diane. She managed to keep her desk fairly clean and organized and seldom looked over at Diane's disorderly desk so she didn't feel anxious about it.

While her computer booted up, she thumbed through the Connert file. The file was organized by home visit notes, financial and employment verifications, and the list of children that had lived at the house. Hadleigh first flipped to the section on their finances and saw, sadly, what she expected to see. Melvyn Connert worked as the finance processor or coordinator at Top End Automotive and had for many years. Nothing remarkable stood out about him or his time at the dealership. He was a good employee, didn't call in sick, would work overtime if it was necessary, and was generally pleasant with customers.

Bethany Connert had worked as a grocery store clerk when they first applied to be foster parents ten years ago. As soon as they got their first foster child, she quit work to stay home and be with the kids. Every kid they'd placed with the Connerts had done well in school. Learned to make money on their own. Learned to cook at least some meals, and only the older kids were taught basic life skills like doing laundry and basic hygiene. The babies were always healthy and every home visit seemed as though they were a dream family. Bethany never seemed frazzled, the house was always clean, and so were the kids.

Melvyn didn't make a ton of money but he made enough to make the mortgage payments and utilities and a modest car payment. The money they received for the foster care of the children seemed to pay for the groceries, things for the kids like school pictures, membership dues for team sports when the child had promise, and other basics. The family didn't take vacations and Melvyn's only outside activity seemed to be bowling on a league during the season. They had no credit cards.

The more Hadleigh looked through the file the more confused she became. There was absolutely nothing noteworthy in this file and certainly no explanation about how they could afford an Escalade.

She heard someone walk into the office and, soon after, the phone rang. Her colleague answered it then her phone buzzed on her desk.

"Hadleigh, a Donovan Keach is on line one for you."

Donovan was calling her? Now that was certainly interesting and exciting. Though not because she wanted to hear from him. Just because he was letting her in. That was the only reason for sure.

Donovan waited anxiously on the phone for Hadleigh to answer. Shaking his head, he scoffed at his feelings and vowed to set them aside. Sure, she was beautiful and smart. There were lots of women like that around. He worked with several of them here.

"Hello?"

Her voice startled him and he quickly cleared his throat.

"Um, morning. This is Donovan. I wondered if you had any luck with the financial records on the Connerts? I'm about to go and nose around Top End Automotive and wanted to be armed with any information you had before-hand so I could ask some questions."

"Good morning." Her voice sounded clear and fresh; he could picture her in his mind and he liked what he saw. "I'm sitting here with their file now and nothing pops up as suspicious. It's just the weirdest thing."

Donovan grinned to himself as he imagined Hadleigh sitting at a desk poring over the Connert information, her intelligent brown eyes scanning pages as she bit her bottom lip.

"Okay, well I'll go in and just ask general questions. Maybe I can get him to feel sorry for me and offer me some sort of a way to make money. That would certainly be a bonus and I'll start with that in mind."

"That's a good idea." He heard her take a deep breath. "I started an online profile last night and made contact with Marco48. He told me I'd be able to make a lot of money if I was willing to pose nude."

Van's heart raced at the emotions rioting through his mind at the thought of Hadleigh posing nude, of her slender body lying on a furry rug while he feasted his eyes on her. He loved the idea and his palms grew sweaty. Then reality snapped into his mind just as quickly and the thought of perverts on the internet looking at her beautiful nude body pissed him off. The abrupt swing in his emotions jarred him.

"What did..." He had to clear his throat. "What did you tell him?"

"I told him I would do anything to make money."

Anything? She'd do anything? Sweet Jesus. His body shook a bit and he inhaled deeply and let it out slowly a few times to get himself under control.

"What was his response to that?"

Her voice softened and she seemed disappointed. "Nothing. He didn't respond at all."

"Did he ask for a picture?" This time Van walked into his living room and stared at the cover of a car magazine on the coffee table to keep himself focused on this conversation.

"He did and I found one of me and my cousin, Hannah, when we were nine, I think. That's when he told me I could make a lot of money."

"Shit." Van mumbled but Hadleigh heard him.

"He has no way of knowing it's me. I used HanMarn as my profile name."

Scraping his hand through his hair, Van stood and paced his living room.

"Hadleigh, please don't do this. Please don't put yourself in a position to get caught and certainly don't jeopardize our investigation."

"I just wanted to know how easy it was to get the attention of some scumbag and since I had his screen name, I messaged him."

"So now you know it's easy. These guys are sick. They are also dangerous. Please don't make contact with him anymore. Can you do that for me?"

"What's in it for me? I want him off the streets."

"We're working on it, I promise."

"But it's taking a long time. In the meantime, how many kids is he using?" Her voice trembled and she took a deep breath.

"That's the absolute hardest part of doing a thorough investigation. But we know that if we don't do a good job of collecting evidence and making sure any charges from police will stick, not only will he slip through the cracks, but he'll be harder to catch next time because he'll be wary."

"I don't know..." Her voice trailed off and he longed to console her.

"Would you like to have dinner with me?"

His voice cracked and he closed his eyes. Partly because he didn't really mean to ask her, but then again he did and worried she'd say no. He held his breath. It seemed like an eternity for her to respond but she finally did.

"Yes. That would be nice."

He let his breath out and felt relieved instantly.

"Great. How about I pick you up at seven and we'll go out to eat somewhere. You pick the restaurant."

"Okay."

"In the meantime, don't make contact with Marco48. Promise."

She hesitated and he was about to ask again when she finally agreed. "Okay."

Her soft voice rang through his head as he said good-bye and then made his way to meet Charly in the conference room and see what Caiden was able to pull together for him last night.

On the ride downstairs, he gave his head a good shake and mumbled to himself how stupid he was being. He just wanted to occupy Hadleigh so she didn't go off and kill his investigation. Charly stood at the conference table studying the large computer screen above Piper's head which displayed a map of the Connerts' street. Charly turned and smiled. "Good morning."

"Morning."

He stood next to Charly. "What's going on?"

"Piper is showing me where they placed cameras last night. We have two more on the Connerts' house and should be able to get some better footage."

"That's great. Did anything come in last night?"

18

Hadleigh's phone alerted her to an email. Taking a deep breath and slowly letting it out, she opened her email program and glanced at the newly arrived email. Marco48.

She sat up straight, swallowed then clicked on the email to open it.

Marco48: "When are you able to have your photo taken? You need to make sure it's a time your foster family won't be suspicious of your absence. I suspect it will take around an hour. Maybe a bit longer."

Oh, she was so excited. He'd responded. That part of it was a weird satisfaction that she was worthy. How gross was that? She didn't need or want to feel worthy of a fucking pedophile pornographer. But, then again, she did. If only to try and help Van and Charly catch this disgusting animal. She started typing out her email. "I think I can meet you tomorrow during the school day. I'll skip out of my PE class."

She was about to send it when she remembered that Van had asked her not to have further contact with him. She sat back in her chair and stared at her email. If she wanted to argue the point, he made contact with her, not the other way around; she was just responding. And maybe Van would be mad, but if she could also make a case here, in writing, that Marco48 was willing to pay her for nude photographs, when they did arrest him, she'd have more proof to help lock him away. Ultimately, that was the goal.

She clicked "send."

Letting out a long breath, she got up and walked out of her tiny office to the coffee machine down the hall to expend the extra adrenaline that rushed through her body. Her hands shook and her knees felt slightly wobbly, so after filling her coffee cup, she continued walking around the office to see who was in. Uninterested in actually engaging in conversation, she decided to head back to her office and get ready for her first home visit of the day.

Her officemate walked in, a weak smile on her face, then she plopped into her desk chair. Plopped was the only way to describe it. Diane was in her mid-fifties, about fifty pounds overweight and walked as if she carried the world on her shoulders. Most of the senior social workers did, and Hadleigh once again reminded herself to get out before her posture changed to one of a slumped-over downtrodden matron. Seeing so many kids throughout your life have so many issues and deal with so much was an enormous burden. Luckily, Hadleigh still held the belief that she was doing good for the kids she placed and was helping them. Many of the social workers, like Diane, had passed that threshold and gone on to a "what else would I do with my life?" phase of their careers and she often wondered how effective they were at this point in the game. But the fact that there weren't loads of social workers knocking on their door to join them kept many of them from leaving. Who would help the kids?

"Good morning." Hadleigh greeted.

"Morning Hadleigh. Busy day for you?"

"Yeah. How about you?"

"Yes. I have a runaway. We're looking for her but she's nowhere to be found and she's been gone for more than twenty-four hours now."

"Oh no. Do you have leads?"

Diane pulled a file off the stack of files on her desk and opened it. "Not many. She was last seen at the Dip N' Twist, a little ice cream shop on Third Avenue, I guess around eight-thirty Sunday night. We had to wait the twenty-four-hour period before police could get involved and now they're looking around for her."

"Oh, Diane, I'm so sorry to hear this. Has she had troubles before?"

"Not really. She's a twelve-year-old girl who has the usual twelve-year-old issues. There was an issue at the home she was in a few weeks ago where another girl accused her of stealing a necklace. She adamantly denied stealing it and the house mother and I went through the girls' bedroom and looked for it. No necklace was found and the mother said she'd never seen either girl with it. But it rattled Janine and since then she's been sullen and edgy."

Hadleigh's heart hurt for the little girl. Sadly, things like this happened all the time. The kids started fights for no reason, usually to get another child in trouble because it made them feel more important or superior. These kids had so little; few possessions and the constant worry of having to move to another family was always on their mind. Birth parents were in and out of their lives, school was often a struggle, and unfortunately, some homes were just better than others. Something she had learned over the years. And now, she was beginning to see that even when you thought you had a good home, things could be deceiving.

"I'll keep a look out while I'm out and about today. Do you have a picture?"

Diane turned to a separate section of the file and pulled a photograph of Janine from an envelope.

"This was taken just three months ago and is still accurate. She was last seen wearing a pair of jeans, sneakers that had been white at one time but now are fairly scuffed and dirty, and a dark blue hoodie."

"Thanks Diane, I'll keep my eyes open for her."

"We need all the help we can get. Foster parents are upset of course, but you know how it is, they have others to take care of and can't spend a lot of time looking for a girl who doesn't want to be found."

"Yes, sad to say I do know how it is."

Hadleigh packed up her belongings, her files ,and her phone and headed out the door for the day with a heavier heart than she'd had just a half hour before. But still hopeful that she'd make a difference today. A good one.

19

Donovan pulled into Hadleigh's driveway and parked. Walking up to the front door, he was oddly excited for his date with Hadleigh. Earlier today he'd tried to remember the last time he'd had an honest to goodness real date and for the life of him he couldn't think of one.

One last swipe of his palms on his thighs before he knocked on the door and his heart hammered in his chest. He shook his head and silently admonished himself for being foolish.

The door opened and there she stood; her long dark blonde hair floated in waves over her shoulders. The sun still partially lit the sky, though it was fading and her hair glistened where the sun touched it. Her lips were shiny and when she smiled it nearly took his breath away. She wore a tight-fitting white dress with a detailed folding of material between and around her breasts and it was hard not to look at them. The dress that is. She was quite simply stunning.

"Hi Donovan, please come in."

"Van. Call me Van."

She smiled and nodded then stepped back to allow him to enter her home and his legs felt weak. She wore white heels which made her already fabulous legs look impossibly long and lean. What he wasn't able to see was molded by the formfitting dress she wore and he felt like a silly teenager on his first date. His nerves hit overdrive, leaving him tongue-tied and unable to say anything.

Happily, Hadleigh spoke to end the silence. "I wasn't sure if you wanted to have a drink first or take off right away. I thought maybe we could go out to Reggie's on the lake."

He cleared his throat. "Reggie's sounds great. I've never been but heard about it. Should we just head over now?"

"Sure, let me grab my purse."

Hadleigh walked away from him and he had the perfect view of her shapely ass; firmly rounded and the perfect size. Van waited until she was around the corner before turning to look out the large front window to get his body under control. He took several slow, calming breaths and reminded himself he'd done this plenty of times before. He was simply rusty and it would all come back to him soon. At least that's how he got himself to relax.

Her heels clicked on the hardwood floors and he turned as she entered the room. "You look stunning Hadleigh."

She smiled at him then. A bright, happy smile that lit up her whole face. He nearly dropped to the floor.

"You look very handsome. But you've looked handsome every time I've seen you, so there's that."

He felt his cheeks and the tips of his ears heat up. He wasn't used to compliments and was rendered speechless for a moment.

"Thank you."

He held his hand out toward the door and she preceded him. Van refused to look at her ass as it swayed in front of him; he watched her hair swish instead.

After he stepped out the door, he turned and tugged it closed.

"Do you need to lock it?"

"Yes," she pulled her keys from her purse and he took them from her, allowing his fingers to brush hers. It felt electric, just that little touch.

He saw her lips tremble and felt better that she felt it too. Now they were on a more even playing field.

After he locked up, they walked to his SUV. After she lifted her legs and swung inside, he closed the door and walked around the front of the vehicle. Once situated inside he started his SUV and looked over at her.

"Do you have directions or an address? We can enter it in my GPS." He handed her his phone with the open app and Hadleigh quickly entered the address.

They drove to the restaurant, and as small talk filled the time, he began to relax. Once seated at the restaurant, he felt a sense of relief to have made it this far.

"I haven't had an honest to goodness date in so many years I couldn't remember it today." He confessed.

Hadleigh looked across the table at him and smiled. "It's been a while for me too. I'm generally busy with work and I don't go out to clubs to party so I guess it keeps me off the market as they say."

He chuckled.

Her phone lit up. She looked at the screen as it lay on the table and he saw her swallow. Then she looked at him and her cheeks flushed bright pink.

"Everything alright?"

"Yes." She shook her head which was contradictory to a yes answer; he watched her closely and waited to see if she'd say anything else.

Their waitress came to the table, told them of the nightly specials, gave them each a drink menu and said she'd be back in a couple of minutes.

Donovan looked at the drink menu. Since he was visually impaired with only one good eye, and adding alcohol to the mix wasn't a great idea, he opted for a white soda.

Hadleigh's phone lit up again just as the waitress left with their orders.

She casually flipped it over so it was face down and he looked her in the eye.

"If you need to respond, go ahead. Believe me I understand having to answer calls."

She bit her bottom lip again and he was unable to look away from her.

"I don't need..." She inhaled and let it out slowly. "Marco48 is trying to set up a meeting with me."

His jaw clenched tightly as he studied her. "Hadleigh, why are you still communicating with him?"

"Because I thought the closer I came to getting to meet him, the more of a paper trail I'd have when you catch him and put him away."

"But..." He stopped then reached across the table to touch her hand. "Don't meet him."

"I won't. I couldn't anyway. I'm not nine."

"And you said you wouldn't contact him anymore either."

"I won't. I mean, only to set a date and time."

"But when are you telling him you can meet?"

"Tomorrow after two because I'm supposed to be in math class."

He started to pull his hand away but she turned her hand up and tucked her fingers in his.

20

A fter he brought her home, she handed him her house keys. He unlocked and opened the door, stepping aside to allow her to enter before following her inside. He was a gentleman through and through, and over their meal, her admiration of him had grown with each passing minute. He was responsible, dependable, tender, and sweet.

She turned to face him; even with her heels on she was several inches shorter than he was. She didn't want to make this weird yet she wasn't sure what to do next. She wanted to kiss him.

He walked into her space, wrapped his arms around her body and pulled her in tightly to him. He dipped his head and his lips touched hers. At first it was a light nip, but he tilted his head slightly and their lips locked. Soft, smooth, sweet kisses, their lips met and moved and molded to each other for long moments.

He pulled away briefly, lay his forehead on hers and softly said, "Every time you bite your bottom lip, I want to kiss you."

"I don't bite my bottom lip."

"Yes, you do. You bite it. Often."

She wrapped her arms around his shoulders and initiated another kiss, because, holy hell, that last one was fantastic.

It did not disappoint. Not even a little. Their lips danced with each other, tongues slid inside each other's mouths, heavy breathing filled the air and she enjoyed every danged minute of it. He felt fantastic against her body. His strength surrounded her and she felt safe and secure and protected. She liked that. She had always had to be her own protector.

He stepped back after a few minutes. Van's eyes peered deeply into hers and he grinned.

"I'd better get going. You have to work tomorrow. But, don't meet with Marco48. Call it off. Tell him something came up and ask him to meet you next week if you must."

"Okay." It came out breathlessly, not convincing at all.

"Hadleigh. Promise me."

She straightened her shoulders and stepped back so she could look into his eyes without having to tilt her head back so far.

"I promise."

"Do I need to be with you around two to make sure?"

"You don't have to, but you can if you want to."

He chuckled then. "Where are you supposed to meet him?"

She pulled her phone from her purse and looked through the emails she'd gotten from him. Her heart hammered in her chest and her vision dimmed. Her hands began to shake and when she looked up at Van, the expression on his face told her he saw something was wrong.

"What is it? Don't hold anything back."

"He wants to meet at the Dip N' Twist. My office mate, Diane, had a runaway and that was the last place they'd seen her."

"When?"

"Sunday night."

"Are the police working on it?"

"Yes, the twenty-four-hour hold was up last night and they still hadn't seen her so they are now searching." She felt numb. Things kept coming at her. So many weird coincidences; the Connerts and now the ice cream shop. Her head swirled.

Van wrapped his arm around her shoulders and led her to the sofa.

"You should sit down, you look like you're about to fall over."

"I'm not."

"I said you look like you might. Just sit." She allowed him to walk her to the sofa, partly because she liked being tucked into the side of his body with his strong arm wrapped around her. The security she felt nestled into him, calmed her.

They sat together, his arm squeezed around her shoulders again and she lay her head back and closed her eyes.

"What are the odds of this?"

She heard as he inhaled, the soft rise and fall of his chest next to her was the only movement he made.

"There seem to be many similarities between the parties we're watching and the places that are now coming to light."

"So, what does that mean?"

"It could mean that we're getting close to finding out who this is for sure. It could mean that events are escalating. Which makes me wonder why? Are we looking at the wrong person with Melvyn? I'm waiting for more information on Brent Jennings since he just came to town and events are escalating, I'm going to give him a closer look. That doesn't explain Melvyn and Bethany's sudden influx of money but it might have been a gift from Brent, something I'll ask Piper or Caiden to check out for me."

She sat forward and twisted so she could meet his gaze.

"I never thought of that. What if Brent did give them some money? Why? Why would he?"

Van's shoulders lifted and fell in a shrug. "I don't know. I know nothing about either of them. Do you? Are they close? Did Brent borrow money at one time and is now paying it back? Did Brent invest money for them at one time and has now cashed out for them?"

"Wow, you really are good at this. I've never considered any of that."

"Hadleigh, it's my job."

"Right, but still, I'm embarrassed that I didn't think of any of that."

"I'll ask Piper and Caiden to research investments in Brent and or Bethany's names to see if something shows up. I'll also ask them to research the LLC that the house is in and Bethany inherited. Maybe at one time it had money that was invested."

"But why would Melvyn have said that his wife saved for the Cadillac if they had inheritance or investments?"

"Maybe he doesn't know. You said he was hands off. Maybe he's really hands off. As in, he doesn't bother with any of it."

Van's voice was soft and smooth when he asked, "Do you think you can get me some information about the girl your friend has missing? I want to see if there are any similarities with any of our situations."

21

V an walked out of the conference room on Wednesday morning ready to tackle the day. Piper was working on the items he'd requested and now he was going to the Dip N' Twist to see if anything stuck out as weird for him.

His phone vibrated and he swiftly pulled it from his back pocket as he waved his watch in front of the elevator panel. The door slid open and he stepped in, pushed the up arrow and checked the text he'd received.

Hadleigh: "I have some information on Janine, the twelve-year-old who ran away."

His fingers tapped out a return message to Hadleigh even as his heart beat a bit faster at receiving a text from her.

"I'm on my way to the Dip N' Twist right now. Want an ice cream?"

Today was looking up and he was going to get this pedophile soon, he could feel it in his bones.

"I'm on my way."

He couldn't help the smile that appeared on his face after reading her message. Today was absolutely looking up.

His phone pinged a few times with incoming texts but couldn't check them as he drove. The ice cream shop wasn't that far away.

He pulled into the parking lot then looked around for Hadleigh's car. Seeing only two other cars in the lot, he decided to wait for her inside. That was after he read the texts that were pinging his phone.

Information from Piper on JenMark LLC; the Connerts inherited LLC. No viable assets, just some old memorabilia worth around $10,000, all since sold.

As he opened the door a bell rang and a young girl popped up from behind the counter and smiled at him.

"Hi, do you need a minute to look at the menu?" She pointed above her where a large black board was hung listing their ice cream flavors, sundaes, and shakes.

"Yes, thank you."

He glanced around the empty shop and figured someone was in the kitchen to account for the second car in the lot. The young girl bustled around filling napkin holders, sprinkle containers, checking various ice cream machines, and generally getting ready for the day.

"What time does it get busy here?" he asked.

She stopped her frenzied moving about and smiled. "Any minute now. At ten we have a group of older guys who come in and have coffee on Wednesdays. They sit at that table over there." She pointed to a larger table in the corner.

Van turned to see the table already set with place settings and coffee cups turned upside down.

"Then at eleven, the lunch crowd starts to drift in."

"You serve lunch here?"

"Just the basics. Hot dogs and hamburgers. We tried a larger menu a while ago, but it didn't go over. So, we're back to simple is better."

Van was impressed with her knowledge. "How long have you worked here?"

She laughed. "My whole life. My parents own this place. I'm twenty-one now and work here when I'm not in school. It'll be mine one day, or so I'm told."

Van nodded. Wow, she didn't look twenty-one and that made him feel old. He would have guessed her for sixteen easy.

The bell rang and he turned to see Hadleigh, fresh as a newly picked peach, walk through the door. Her long blonde hair hung over her shoulders in waves, her lips gleamed where the light hit them, her sexy legs were encased in dark blue jeans, tight at the ankle, and she wore a pair of open-toe shoes with a slight heel on them. She looked posh, svelte and sexy as hell. His body roared to life as she walked toward him, a smile on her face, a twinkle in her eye.

"Good morning." She purred when she was close enough to touch. So, he did.

He leaned in and kissed her shiny lips, his hands each snaked around her waist to pull her in close.

"Good morning." He rasped in return.

A noise from behind the counter had Hadleigh turning toward the younger woman watching them. Hadleigh smiled at her. "Hello."

"Hi. Take your time." The girl smiled back as she started another pot of coffee.

Hadleigh looked up at him, her lips parted in the sweetest smile.

"It's nice to see you."

His breathing hitched up a bit. "It's nice to see you too."

He took her hand to lead her to the counter. "What will you have?"

Hadleigh studied the menu briefly. "I'll have a medium chocolate waffle cone."

"You didn't have to study that long."

Giggling, she responded. "Nope. Chocolate custard is my favorite, there's never a decision to be made."

"Good to know."

Waiting for the young lady to take their order, he squeezed Hadleigh's hand in his and embraced feeling like a teenager again. It had been such a long time.

"Have you two decided?"

Van ordered for them. "Yes, two medium chocolate custard waffle cones."

"You got it."

He let go of Hadleigh's hand only long enough to pull his wallet from his back pocket and lay a ten-dollar bill on the counter. He tucked his wallet away, then promptly took her hand in his again.

"So, what are we going to do while we're here?" She asked.

He turned to face her, lowered his voice and whispered. "I thought we'd sit over in that corner and eat our ice cream, while we watch the comings and goings of customers and employees. I'm watching especially for unusual activity, young girls coming in and either loitering without eating, looking to meet someone, or just going to the back and not returning."

"Here you go."

Van reached forward and took the cones then nodded to the ten on the counter. "Keep the change," he added. Since the cones were $3.50 each it would leave her a decent tip.

He walked Hadleigh to a table at the back of the shop, it sat on the opposite end of the room from where the men would be gathered, and expected to sit for a while.

22

Hadleigh watched Van and grew more impressed with him than she'd been last night. His eyes, or eye, was always keen to what was going on around them as he enjoyed his ice cream cone. A group of older gentlemen came in and sat across the room from them, enjoying coffee and ooh boy did they gossip. She half listened as she also watched a group of younger girls come in, get a small cone and sit at a table in the center of the room. Clearly looking to be seen, which made her sad.

"That makes me feel so bad. Those girls are looking to be noticed and that behavior seldom brings about good attention."

"You didn't do that when you were their age?"

"No. I mean..." She thought about it a bit but the need to be noticed was never something she'd felt. "No. My friends and I were usually at some practice or another. Cheer-leading practice. Band practice. Choir practice. I was always busy doing something. Especially after my cousin, Hannah, and Aunt Marnie were killed."

"How were they killed?" He stared intently at her, genuinely interested in her response.

She swallowed the last of her ice cream cone and wiped her lips with a white napkin pulled from the metal holder on the table.

"My Uncle Joshua killed them." Sorrow filled her. "I haven't said his name since the day he killed them."

Van's hands slid across the tabletop and wrapped around hers.

"Do you want to tell me what happened?"

She didn't. But then again, she did. She inhaled, blinking away the threatening tears. "He was abusing Hannah. She never told me. We were so close. Almost inseparable actually. Aunt Marnie was my mom's sister and we did everything together, the four of us girls. When Hannah was nine, I noticed that she began to withdraw from me. Even her beautiful face changed. She smiled less. She stopped laughing at silly things girls laugh at. She started wearing baggy clothing that hid her body. She tried to be invisible."

Van's hands squeezed hers, his eyes looked into hers, but he sat silently waiting for her to finish.

"When we were eleven and started getting larger breasts, she really became withdrawn. She cried a lot and I tried to get her to tell me what was wrong. She always wanted me to sit with her but not say anything. She never wanted me to come to their house anymore. Then I overheard my mom telling my dad that something was wrong with Aunt Marnie. Mom saw bruises on Aunt Marnie's arms and legs. When she asked, Aunt Marnie said she was just so clumsy."

Hadleigh took a moment to swallow, take a drink of the glass of water they had at the table, and take another deep breath.

"Then one day Aunt Marnie called my mom crying. She finally said that she'd caught Uncle Joshua raping Hannah. He'd beaten both of them and told them not to say anything. He was a minister. He thought no one would believe them anyway. And that they were too stupid to be believed." Then Uncle Joshua caught Aunt Marnie on the phone and began beating her with it while my mom listened. My dad was so mad he went over there and found Aunt Marnie and Hannah beaten to death, the bloody phone handset hanging from the phone covered in blood. He'd fled the house but Dad ran to a neighbor's and called the police. They found Uncle Joshua hiding in the church."

Van lifted her hands and kissed her fingers while he looked into her eyes. "I'm so very sorry for your loss, baby."

Her heart pounded in her chest. She'd only told one other person in her life about Aunt Marnie and Hannah and that was Lucy. But also, Van called her baby. She'd never in her life been called baby and it made her feel special. She felt like she could fly right now.

Tears sprang to her eyes and one instantly slid down her cheek. Van was quick to reach over with the back of his forefinger and wipe it away. He pulled a clean handker-chief from his back pocket and unfolded it for her.

"It's clean." He smiled as she gratefully took it in her hands and dabbed at her tears and gently wiped her nose.

"Thank you." She cleared her throat. "I've only told one other person that story."

His voice was soft, gentle and soothing when he replied. "I'm honored you trusted me with it."

She managed a smile and took a deep breath.

"Is that why you wanted to be a social worker?"

She nodded. "I thought if I'd seen the signs sooner maybe we could have done something to prevent it. At least the murders. But when he was questioned, Joshua said he'd only at first began touching her. He didn't rape her right away, so maybe I could have seen the signs and stopped her from being raped."

Van swallowed and sat upright in his chair, but he never let go of her hands. "You likely wouldn't have been able to stop it, baby. These men, these gross perverts are so good at what they do. It's sick to think that calling them good at it is a way to describe them, but they know what they're doing is wrong. They know they have to keep it hidden and they know they have to control their victims so they don't tell. Usually they begin with months, or sometimes years, of grooming."

She nodded, "I know on some level you're right. On another level, I want to believe I can prevent it from happening to any other young girl."

"Then, let's get Marco48 and if we can, any accomplices he has. That's how we have to do it. One pedophile at a time. One trafficker at a time. If we're diligent and stay positive and keep our eyes on the mission, we'll clean up these assholes."

She smiled at him. "That sounds perfect. Yes, that's what I want to do."

23

H adleigh went back to work and Donovan stayed at the Dip N' Twist to watch the players. The players being anyone looking suspicious, anyone seemingly interested in anything nefarious, anyone, period, who seemed out of place.

Usually people involved in criminal enterprise were very good at hiding themselves as a criminal, but Donovan, and his co-workers, were very good at spotting even the best actors.

Van ordered some fries and tried to remain inconspicuous to anyone coming and going. He texted Charly and Caiden so they knew he was working and Charly responded that she'd be around in a bit to see what was going on.

The older men in the corner were still chatting away. The gal behind the counter brought them fresh pots of coffee and a few of them ordered sundaes, or cones or a burger.

As she brought them the last of their food orders, she approached his table.

"Anything else I can get you?"

He smiled at her. "Not now, but I have a co-worker coming in soon and then we'll order lunch."

"Sounds good. My name is Alison if you need anything in the meantime."

She gave him a saucy smile and for the first time in a long time he enjoyed being flirted with. But, he wasn't interested. In a very short amount of time, Hadleigh had gotten his attention and he was not only puzzled by that, but amused by it. It had been a long while since he'd been with someone in an actual relationship and he'd forgotten how special that felt. To have someone to trust and be trusted by, but also that special someone that you could talk to and share things with.

His phone rang and he answered it without looking at the read out.

"Keach."

"Really? That's how you answer your phone?"

He chuckled. "Yes, it's how I answer my phone when I don't know who's calling. Had I known it was you I would have said, 'What's up dickhead?'"

His brother, Daniel, laughed on the other end of the phone. "It's scary how similar we are brother. I was about to say the same to you but you caught me off guard with the Keach."

"It's how I answer work calls to be more specific."

"Can you talk now or are you working?"

"Both. I'm working, but I can talk. What's up with you?"

"Work's a grind, the weather here in Oregon sucks ass and I broke up with Michelle."

"That's a whole load of bullshit going on right there. What's wrong, aren't the nurses playing nice with the doctors anymore?"

"Fuck off."

Van chuckled. "Anything I can do?"

"I'm thinking about a vacation to Indiana to spend time with my brother. Would you mind a visitor?"

"Not at all. I'd love to see you."

"This weekend?"

"Things must be bad, but you got it. Let me know when your flight lands and I'll pick you up."

"It's a plan. See you Saturday. Maybe Friday night. You have a date or anything?"

Van chuckled. "Not at this minute, but I might. Want me to bring one for you?"

"Yeah. Do that. Make sure she's hot, fun, and easy."

Van groaned, Dan could be a dog and right now he was likely fucking his way through a string of women after his breakup. That meant he wouldn't be bringing any of his co-workers along. Once Dan had finished his residency and got his job at a large hospital, he'd relished being idolized by basically everyone, including his parents. While

Van, who went off to war and was wounded to boot, was the bad boy with the tattoos, surly attitude, and had left all his potential on the table to shoot at people and be shot at. Despite it all, he and Dan remained close.

"I'm only promising the hot part. Maybe the fun part, but you're not fucking your way through my coworkers or any of Hadleigh's friends."

"Oh, Hadleigh, now that's interesting. You don't have a date, or not yet, but you know who it will be with, and you're already protecting her. I can't wait to meet Hadleigh and hear all about this relationship."

"You may not get to hear about it at all. It's my personal business. Just get your head on straight and let me know when you're flying in."

Dan laughed on the other end and then just hung up. Typical.

The bell over the door rang again and Van looked up expecting to see Charly. Instead he saw Brent Jennings. Trying not to be too obvious, Van pulled his phone up and snapped a couple of pictures of Brent as he spoke to Alison at the counter. She seemed flirty with him; he leaned one hip against the counter and crossed his arms as he chatted with her. After a few minutes, she cocked her head, said something to Jennings and then he walked to the end of the counter and she led him to a back room where they disappeared.

He texted his pictures to Piper and Caiden, who were working on compiling information on Jennings and on the LLC his parents had passed down to Bethany if not both of them: JenMark.

The bell chimed again and Charly walked through and straight to him. The old men across the room turned to watch Charly walk toward him, most of them with devilish smiles on their faces, a couple of them with their mouths hanging open.

That was the thing about Charly; she was stunning. Short blonde curly hair, petite frame, light blue eyes, and a gorgeous smile. She had a vivacious personality, a quick wit, and a wicked sense of humor. But, ooh, she was smart, cunning, and she didn't take any shit from anyone. People naturally gravitated to her and usually it took them a long time to notice that she had a prosthetic left arm because they were too busy looking at her face or her body. She worked out religiously and she didn't let her lack of one arm stop her from doing anything. That was the case now. The men in the corner were watching her saunter across the floor and she smiled brightly and waved with her right arm at them. Some of them waved back, a couple of them had mouths gaping open and one of them clapped, to which she stopped a few feet from them, bowed at the waist and saucily quipped, "Good afternoon, gentlemen." Before turning and walking to his table.

Van laughed and looked her in the eye. "You do know how to command a room Charly."

24

H adleigh walked into the office with a spring in her step.

"Well, look at you, what has you in such a chipper mood this morning?"

Diane was already slugging through files to pull the ones she'd need for the day.

"I'm just in a good mood, that's all."

Diane harrumphed but kept shifting the stacks of files on her desk. "Give me some of that would you?"

"Still haven't found your runaway?"

"No. Not a trace."

"It's so weird that a person can disappear without a trace. There must be a trail. Somewhere there has to be a trail."

Diane stood and hefted her heavy satchel over her shoulder. "The problem here is she's a foster kid. No parents in the picture at all and the foster parents only had her a couple of months. No real bonds holding her to anyone. Meaning that I'm likely the person who cares the most about her. Sad but true. I did go out last night and looked at some of the hiding places she'd told me about; where she'd hung out when she needed time or space, but no sign of her."

"I'm sorry Diane. I'd love to help you. What can I do?"

As she stepped into the hall Diane responded, "You know anyone who can track down a missing teen?"

Diane disappeared and Hadleigh smiled. As a matter of fact, she did and she was going to see him later tonight.

Hadleigh invited Van to her house for dinner, something she was incredibly excited about. She'd make him a big meal and hopefully get some information from him, and if things progressed as they had been, maybe enjoy more of his kisses and her stomach tingled with thoughts of what more they could lead to. She was beginning to enjoy her time with him immensely. It didn't hurt that he was incredibly attractive. Handsome in that rugged, tattooed, bad boy sort of way, but he was anything but a bad boy. After all, he saved kids. How bad could you be if your job was, first and foremost, saving kids from life, pedophiles, traffickers, themselves?

Her phone pinged a text and she excitedly looked at it hoping to see a text from Van. Her stomach rolled when she saw Marco48 instead.

Rolling her head on her shoulders before opening the text, she then took a deep breath and tapped on the text.

"You didn't respond. Meet me at the Dip N' Twist at nine-thirty tonight?"

Van had asked her to put it off until next week. She'd also promised she would. But what if this was the only chance to meet with him and catch him? Still, she had plans tonight and putting it off for one more day couldn't hurt. Also, she didn't want to seem too anxious.

Hadleigh replied, "I have some crap with the foster mom tonight. Can't get out of it. Tomorrow?"

She tapped send and let out a breath. Then she began pulling her files for the day's home visits and noted that one of them took her close to the Connerts. She'd take a detour and drive by in hopes she'd see something that helped her out in this matter.

Throwing her large file-filled satchel over her shoulder, Hadleigh turned off the light and headed toward her car.

Her phone chimed a text as she climbed into her car. Pulling her phone from her bag she noted Marco48's text.

"Tomorrow works. Ten thirty pm. I have plans earlier."

She typed out her response, "k."

She did put him off, but not until next week. She'd tell Van tonight and let him know why she was concerned about waiting until next week. After all, he said he'd set up a meeting for tomorrow for himself, so she'd likely never have to meet with him anyway.

As she drove to her first home for a visit, she tried to mentally get herself in the game. This was a family with two kids placed by her. Both kids were high school age, the worst for foster kids. They found more things to get into and it was usually because they knew they'd be aging out of the system soon and did things out of fear of what would happen to them.

She parked in the driveway of the two-story home just out of the city limits of Lynyrd Station and into a suburb named Lynyrd Valley. It was a nice area of town, more country than city, more farms than stores. This family had been raising foster children for years while also raising their own three kids. They had it figured out.

It was also a hobby farm and both parents did a good job of balancing the kids' schoolwork, farm work, and work ethic so that most of the kids they'd helped raise had done well for themselves outside of foster care. Hadleigh could only think of one over the years that just couldn't get past her own attitude and ended up overdosing on her twentieth birthday. Of course, by that time she was no longer in foster care, but Hadleigh tried keeping track of the kids who aged out of the system. Sadly, this one had been in and out of the hospital often for her drug use.

As Hadleigh walked to the house she looked around the area and inhaled the fresh scent of lilac from the blooming bushes that adorned the property.

Her phone rang and she stopped on the sidewalk and fished her phone from her purse.

She saw Donovan's name and smiled as she answered, "Hi handsome, how are you?"

"I'm rather pissed off, Hadleigh. I thought I asked you to put Marco48 off until next week."

"I did put...I mean you did, but I was afraid I'd lose my chance..."

"You promised me."

"I know, but I did put him off, just until tomorrow. I was going to tell you about it tonight."

"Hadleigh, please don't hamper my investigation. Please stop playing this game you have no idea how to play."

"It's not a game...I'm not afraid." She hated that she stammered.

"Did you call police and ask them to be there so they could arrest him?"

"No, I di...."

"So what are you going to do? Show up there and say, 'Surprise, I'm not nine.'"

"No, I mean I didn't think about it fully..."

"Naw, really? You didn't think about the ramifications of this?"

"Van, I..."

"Call. It. Off."

"How do you even know..."

"Call it off."

Anger bubbled in her like a volcano about to erupt.

"Van, listen..."

"If you let him get away, you aren't saving any child from harm. Do you hear me?"

25

H e was seething. She was going to jeopardize their whole investigation. He didn't lose. Ever.

He set his phone on the table and looked over at Charly, who watched him with a smirk on her face.

"You know you catch more flies with honey, Van."

"She promised me, Charly."

"If you'd just talk to her, without yelling, you'll find out what's happening."

"I wasn't yelling."

"Oookayyy. Well, you weren't inviting conversation."

He scoffed and sat back in his chair. Charly smiled at him and continued. "I think you've got it bad for Hadleigh and this outburst is more from fear of something happening to her than her blowing up our investigation. We have police on standby, we can have them here in two shakes. So, coming in before her tomorrow isn't a deal breaker for us."

"Its...she'll ruin all we worked for."

Charly laughed. "She's gotten your attention. It's good Van, we all should have someone in our lives that's special to us. Don't be pig-headed and fight it."

"I'm not fighting it. I'm just..."

The door opened and a young girl walked into the store with a hooded sweatshirt over her head. She looked at the floor as she walked and stood at the end of the counter where Brent Jennings had so recently disappeared.

Alison walked out, gave her head a quick nod and the girl immediately walked to the back and disappeared behind the door Brent had gone through.

"There's something going on back there. I wonder if there's a window outside I might look into?"

Charly turned toward the door, then back to him. "I'll keep our seats, why don't you go check. Use your camera not your head."

Van quickly stood and walked toward the door, slipping out and walking around the building to the left. Turning to the side of the building he didn't see any windows so he continued on to the back. Once he reached the back of the building, he saw two windows up high on the wall, sort of like basement windows on top. He looked around for something to stand on, hoping to snap some pictures of the inside and what was going on. Locating a few empty crates close to the back door he walked over, and just for the hell of it, checked to see if the back door was locked. The knob turned and clicked and he couldn't believe his luck, it was open.

Looking around to make sure no one was watching, he slipped inside. As soon as the door closed, he waited as his eyes adjusted to the dim light. With only one good eye, that was more essential than ever. Leading the way with his head turned and his right eye forward, Van heard voices in a room to his left. He halted and listened, hoping to hear what they were saying. Nothing discernible.

Inching his way along, he managed to get close to the door but tucked himself behind a stack of empty five-gallon pails. Clattering from the kitchen, which was across the hall from him and down the hall a bit prohibited him from hearing anything.

The bell above the door in the ice cream shop rang and Van tucked himself tighter to the wall. The door opened and Alison walked out, saying, "Just stay in here and I'll bring your food back."

Then he heard Brent tell someone, "Now just stand over there and pretend you're trying to get away." The click of a camera was heard before the door closed.

He may have misjudged Melvyn Connert all along. Brent Jennings was perhaps Marco48. He was in there taking pictures and the only other person he'd seen coming back here was the young girl with the hoodie.

Inching his way down the hall and to the back door he hurried out and leaned against the wall to catch his breath and let his eye adjust to the sunlight.

After a few moments he took a few of the crates and stacked them in an alternating pattern so he had some stability. They weren't that robust and he weighed enough that he'd break through them without some creative stacking.

After making sure the flash on his camera was turned off, he slowly climbed on the crates until his phone rose above the window. He then snapped photos and prayed he'd get something useful.

Voices neared the back of the building and Van scrambled as fast as he could off the crates and ran around to the front of the building, entering just as an older couple stepped inside.

He hurried over to Charly and sat quickly, then opened the photo app on his phone and began looking through the photos he'd just taken.

"Brent Jennings is back there taking pictures of that girl who walked in a while ago with the hoodie on. Alison is bringing them some food back there soon. I'm hoping I got some pictures of what he's taking through the window."

"How did you get all that information?"

"The back door was unlocked. I snuck in and listened."

"Nice work."

"Thanks."

He scrolled through the pictures, noting they were all dark and mostly he got the glare from the sun shining on the window and little else. He could see forms though so he forwarded the pictures to Piper and asked her to see if she could lighten them up.

"Piper's good and so is Caiden. They'll do what they can. I think Deacon is back tomorrow and he can help them with all the information we've asked from them."

"That's good. Anything from them so far on the Connerts and the LLC?"

Charly tapped her phone. "Yes, I just got something."

"So are you two ready to order your lunch?"

He looked up to see Alison standing at the end of the table, looking at the pictures on his phone. Good thing they were hard to decipher.

"Charly, what'll you have?"

"I'm gonna have a burger and can you cut it in half? Then I'll have a cone before I leave."

Alison replied, "Sounds good. And how about you?"

"I'll have the same."

When he looked up Alison's eyes narrowed in suspicion but didn't know if it was directed at him or not.

26

He had no right speaking to her like he'd done. Granted she didn't do as he asked. But still. She was getting more and more pissed as the day wore on and she had a good mind to email Marco48 and tell him she'd meet him tonight just to spite Van.

She drove down the road the Connerts lived on and tried getting her temper under control. As she neared the Connerts' home, she slowed just a bit and watched as Bethany carried some items to the garage. One of the items looked to be a long narrow post or pole. There was a red blanket or sheet on top of a box and the box itself seemed not that heavy, but still not light in weight. Not wanting to seem suspicious, she had to keep driving but she wondered about the items Bethany carried.

Turning to the right at the end of the street, she made another right at the first street and that's when it hit her. That red sheet was the same color as the one in that upper bedroom with the camera. Bethany was hiding it in case she came back for a home visit.

Her heart hammered in her chest and she tried to focus on what she should do next. They were hiding evidence. Melvyn was probably Marco48 and Bethany knew they'd get caught, which meant she knew all about it. Or had she just found out about it when they'd gone up into that room? Her hands began shaking and she wondered how she could get into that garage and see for herself. She couldn't be caught breaking in. Then she thought if she hurried, she could just stop in and see Bethany back there and perhaps step inside and get a close up look for herself.

Pulling into a driveway she carefully backed out of it and pointed her car in the opposite direction. Her throat dried and her heartbeat sped up as she turned left at the end of the street and then another left to turn on to the street the Connerts lived on. She went as fast as she dared and found a space just a few down from the front of the Connerts' home.

Jumping quickly from her vehicle, she walked as fast as her heeled feet would take her without falling and making things worse. As she started up the driveway Bethany saw her and quickly turned to lock the garage door. Hadleigh halted only briefly, failure crawling up her body as she plastered on a smile and continued forward toward Bethany.

"Hi Bethany. How are you?"

Bethany turned and folded her hands in front of her. The look on her face was not the happy look she normally received and Hadleigh knew why.

"I'm fine. What are you doing here again today?"

"I saw you outside and thought I'd stop in. I'm sorry things were left tense between us. I sure don't want that for either of us so I thought I'd stop in and apologize while I was in the area."

The look on Bethany's face barely changed and Hadleigh, for the first time, felt as though she didn't really know Bethany as well as she'd thought.

"I appreciate your apology."

Bethany stood in place, not making any attempt to move and Hadleigh realized her time to get in the garage had passed, but also that any attempt to rectify her previous relationship with Bethany had likely passed as well. That sat like a rock in her stomach as she further realized that every visit from this point forward would be uncomfortable. And the trust, if there had ever really been any, was now lost.

"Okay. Well, that was all I needed to say. I'll see you next week."

Bethany only nodded and stared. Hadleigh turned and slowly walked away, trying to negate the awful feeling that Bethany was staring a hole through her head and wishing all sorts of bad things upon her.

After she turned off the driveway and onto the sidewalk, Hadleigh inhaled deeply and exhaled. Her hands still shook slightly and the adrenaline rush that was bouncing through her body was a bit over-whelming. First Van and now Bethany. Who else was going to nip at her today?

Just as she thought it, she realized she shouldn't have because she'd just invited trouble for herself. What was a way to ward off bad vibes? She needed to find a gem store or some fragranced oils to keep her safe and rid the black energy surrounding her right now.

She got into her car and closed her eyes for a minute. Inhaling and exhaling slowly to calm herself enough to drive safely. That's when her phone rang.

"Hello?" she answered when she saw it was her office calling.

"Hadleigh, this is Lucy. Where are you?"

"Oh Lucy, how is your mom?"

Lucy hesitated briefly, "She's still the same. No change."

"I'm sorry Lucy."

"It happens to all of us eventually. My parents were very pragmatic people and I grew up knowing about life and death. Thank you."

"Again, if there is anything I can do just..."

"Hadleigh were you just at the Connerts'?"

Hadleigh blinked as her brain processed the abrupt change of tone and subject matter.

"Yes, just briefly. I didn't even go inside though."

"Bethany Connert just called and is upset that you popped in unannounced. She doesn't want any more of these surprise visits."

Hadleigh stared out the windshield of her car but saw nothing. Her mind reeled and anger bubbled up inside of her like she'd never felt before. Bethany had called and reported her. Her? It should have been the other way around.

"I just saw her outside carrying things to the garage and so I stopped in to apologize for how things were left the other day. I..."

"Leave her be for a while Hadleigh. She's very upset."

"I am as well Lucy. I should have filed a report yesterday and now I see that was a mistake. She's hiding things."

"If you file the report now it'll look like harassment."

What? What was she hearing just now?

"I'm not harassing her. I...I...just..."

She couldn't even complete a sentence she was so blindsided.

"Come back to the office today and we'll have a chat."

27

Van finished his iced tea and decided he'd loitered here about as long as he could.

"I guess we should go back to the office and see if there is something we can do from there. It's going to look suspicious if we stay any longer. And, admittedly, I'm getting antsy waiting for information to come in."

"I agree. I'll come back here tonight to make sure Hadleigh doesn't come back."

"She won't. She's having dinner with me."

Charly laughed. "See, she's gotten your attention."

Charly stood and pushed her chair in. The older gentlemen in the corner had dwindled to three and they all appreciatively looked over and eyed Charly.

Van also stood and grinned, "Your fan club is watching."

She smiled at him and turned toward the older men. Walking to their table she smiled her brightest smile. "You all have a great day now."

They were rendered speechless as she sauntered away, giving her hips a bit of an extra sway.

After she'd walked out of the store one of the older men looked at Van and said, "You're a lucky man. Not one but two beauties. If I were forty years younger, I'd give you a run for your money though."

Van laughed, "I have no doubt."

He was still smiling as he walked to his car.

Deciding to take a drive past the Connert home, his stomach twisted when he saw Hadleigh's car across the street a couple houses down from the Connerts' home. Pulling to the curb, he shook his head as he stalked across the street and then toward her car. Anger surged through him as he approached and saw her on her phone in the car. His phone rang and he looked down to see Hadleigh's name on the display.

"Yes."

He could see her sitting in her car and continued to walk toward her. "I have to cancel tonight."

"No."

"What?"

"No."

"You can't just tell me no. I can do what I want and..."

He watched her then, still unaware that he was there. She started crying and he saw her wipe her eyes.

"Hadleigh, I'm almost to your car."

She looked up, a bit startled, and hung up the phone. She swiped at her eyes and pulled a tissue from the console of her car and wiped her nose. He opened her passenger door and sat in the passenger seat.

Van took a deep breath and let it out slowly before turning to look at Hadleigh. Her nose was red and her eyes were rimmed in red. They glistened, then a tear fell from her right eye and tracked down her soft cheeks.

He ground his jaw together and thought that even crying she was a beautiful woman.

"Why were you going to cancel dinner tonight?"

"I screwed up."

He clenched his jaw again and focused on even breathing. "How?"

"I'm supposed to be doing a home visit on the next street over now, but as I drove by, I saw Bethany Connert carrying things to the garage. I recognized a red sheet from that upstairs storage room and thought she was hiding the camera in case we came to do an inspection. So, I stopped in. Casual like. Told her I wanted to apologize for leaving things tense between us."

He watched her face. She was clearly shaken and his anger quickly subsided to worry.

"And, what happened?"

"She was cold, but that was it. I told her I'd see her next week and left. I didn't get to see in the garage, but I know that was the sheet I'd found up there. It was used as a backdrop."

He nodded but didn't say anything.

"Anyway, I just got off the phone with my boss who told me that Bethany called her very upset and I'm not allowed to go there and am instructed to finish out my home visits and go back to the office to speak with her."

"You don't think she'll fire you, do you?"

"No, nothing like that. It's just I've never been disciplined. I've always done what was asked of me. I feel bad and mad and frustrated," she huffed.

Van twisted in his seat so he could see her better from his right eye. He watched as she swiped daintily at her nose and dabbed a clean tissue under her eyes. He noticed her hands shaking and felt bad for her. Poor little good girl had just gotten into trouble.

"I understand your frustration."

"No, you don't."

He chuckled which caused her to frown. "Yes, I actually do. I served in the military, and there's little that's as frustrating as military life."

That got a small smile from her. "I suppose that's true."

"It is, believe me. Also, the bad part of my job is the endless waiting. Waiting for information to come through. Waiting for someone to do something that we could finally catch them at. Waiting for gorgeous women to stop impeding my investigations. Endless waiting."

Hadleigh looked up at him; her beautiful shining eyes locked on his. He wasn't able to look away. He saw her swallow, the heat in the car ramped up with them sitting in it and her scent filled his nostrils. He was unable to stop his forward movement as he leaned in and kissed her. Her lips still quivered slightly and they were warm and soft. They felt like satin against his and he enjoyed how they felt against his.

His tongue swiped her lips and she immediately opened her mouth to allow him entry. Her tongue danced with his and he liked that even more. His skin heated and his body responded to her in every way. Pulling away slightly, he kissed the tip of her nose then sat back.

"Go finish your home visits and talk to your boss. You thought you were doing a good thing and if Bethany Connert wasn't guilty of anything, she wouldn't be upset. She's likely just found out that Melvyn or her brother are involved in something nefarious and she's lashing out. It's not you—it's them. Then, expect me at six as planned and if you don't feel like cooking, we'll order in. But we are spending the evening together."

Her eyes locked on his and he saw the change in her expression as a calm settled over her. "I wasn't completely innocent either. I hoped to catch her before she left the garage."

"Leave that part out when you speak to your boss."

Hadleigh nodded and he let out a long breath of air. It was relief more than anything.

"Is this going to hurt your investigation?"

She picked at some invisible lint on her thigh with nervous fingers.

"Not likely. Though there may be some hesitation now on the part of Marco48 if he feels we're getting close. Or more likely that someone is getting close. It might also ramp up his actions to move faster to get out of town before the shit show starts. Time will tell."

She nodded again. "I only put him off till tomorrow."

He placed his fingers under her chin and pulled her face up to look at him.

"I asked you to put him off until next week."

"I know."

"Why?"

"I was afraid he'd get suspicious and say forget it."

"Okay. What time?"

"Ten thirty. He said he had plans earlier."

Van's fingers left Hadleigh's chin, "He does. With me. So you'll not have to meet him at all."

28

Hadleigh pulled the roast out of the oven and set it on the stove. Reaching over it she turned the oven off, pulled her oven mitts off and tucked them in a drawer alongside the stove. She'd let it rest then pull the carrots and potatoes from the inside and slice the roast.

The doorbell rang and she inhaled a deep breath and let it out slowly as she walked to the door. Clearing her throat slightly before opening it, she muttered to herself that all was good. She'd been repeating this over and over since meeting with Lucy.

As she opened the door she smiled, but when she saw Van standing in her doorway, a gorgeous bouquet of coral roses in one hand and a bottle of wine in another, her smile grew.

"Hi, come in."

She stepped back to allow him entry and as he entered his woodsy scent followed him. Goosebumps rose on her arms at his presence in her space.

He turned and handed her the roses, "Beautiful flowers for a beautiful woman."

She reached for them but he held firmly, a sassy smile on his face. She leaned in and kissed his lips and she was glad she did. He was a great kisser.

"I brought this too." He handed her a bottle of wine.

"Wow! You came bearing gifts."

"I did."

She giggled as she took the wine. "Follow me into the kitchen and you can open the wine while I put these in water."

"Deal."

He followed closely behind her and she felt giddy. She tried remembering the last time she'd had a man in her home for a date and in all honesty, she couldn't remember if she ever had anyone special here. When she'd dated previously, they always went out somewhere. In college, she had a boyfriend who always wanted her at his house with all his roommates. Looking back on it, it was gross there, but she was young and, she thought, in love.

"Something smells fantastic."

"Thank you. I made a pot roast for dinner and I bought a cheesecake for dessert."

"That all sounds fantastic."

"Good. And I hope you're hungry because the roast is big and I surely don't want to have to eat leftovers for a week."

He chuckled, which warmed her insides.

"I'll do my best."

Hadleigh pulled a bottle opener from a drawer and handed it to him, then walked across the kitchen to the cupboard next to the refrigerator and pulled out a vase. Van began working on the foil covering over the cork on the wine bottle and she started cutting off the bottoms of the stems and putting the roses in the vase.

As he worked he asked, "How did things go with your boss this afternoon?"

She took a deep breath, happy to have this conversation and get it over with. "It was fine. She's going to take over the Connert account for the time being and I'm taking one of hers. She's hoping that will be the end of it with the Connerts. I didn't tell her anything more about the investigation or our suspicions about them and she didn't ask."

"Okay. Well, that's not too bad."

"No. It still stings a little but it could have been worse."

He held up the bottle of wine and she pointed to a cabinet above the counter where she kept the wine glasses.

She glanced at his back as he reached inside for the glasses and enjoyed the way his muscles played and danced as he moved. He was a hard bodied, smart, handsome man. She could have done so much worse.

He turned and saw her watching him; he smiled.

"I watch you when you aren't looking, too."

Her cheeks heated and her body grew warm. She stared at him and he smiled then he shrugged. She watched as he poured them each a glass of wine then quickly finished placing the roses in the vase. They were stunning.

"I've never gotten coral roses before, they're gorgeous."

"They are my mom's favorite. I wasn't sure what your favorite is so I went with what I knew."

She giggled. "They're perfect. I guess I don't have a favorite color, they're all so beautiful."

He handed her the glass of wine he'd poured, then tapped his glass to hers. "Here's to a fantastic evening."

"Cheers."

She sipped her wine and then set her glass on the counter to take the roast from the pan but Van stepped in front of her.

"I've thought about you all day Hadleigh. I can't seem to not think about you."

Wow, oh wow.

His arms pulled her into his body and her arms immediately wrapped around his shoulders. He bent his knees then lifted her against his body and she naturally wrapped her legs around his hips. His mouth tested and teased hers, their lips fitting together perfectly. His hands slid down her body and cupped her ass. He squeezed and her body exploded into all sorts of feelings. Moisture gathered between her legs, her heartbeat increased and her body grew warm. She'd thought about him every time she had a minute today. Especially after he'd kissed her in her car. Especially after his aftershave lingered in her car and she smelled him all afternoon. After speaking with Lucy, she'd eagerly walked to her car hoping his scent was still inside and was so friggin happy when it was. She'd sat in the warmth of her car inhaling Van's scent and her nipples pebbled tightly while she thought about what it would be like to have sex with him.

His hands now roamed over her body, her back, he squeezed her breasts one at a time as he held her tightly against him. Her mouth eagerly sought his, then kissed along his jaw and his ear and then found his mouth once again as their fevered movements increased in excitement.

She managed to whisper in his ear, "My bedroom is just down the hall."

"Lead the way."

He said it but never set her down. Instead, he carried her as she was wrapped around him and she continued to kiss his neck, his jaw, his ear.

"This one." She mumbled as he approached her bedroom door.

He walked them to the bed, then rather than setting her down, he kneeled on the bed first then gently lay down over her. She kept her legs wrapped around him and now that he didn't have to hang on to her his hands plunged under her blouse and sought her nipples, pinching them tighter, causing her to sigh.

He pushed her blouse and bra up at the same time and his mouth sought her nipples; he hungrily sucked them into his mouth which caused moisture to gather between her legs.

He showered attention on one nipple until it was almost painful; she moaned slightly and his head sought the other one. He nibbled with his teeth, gently but just enough to create a sensation that raced right between her legs. Holy wow, that had never happened before.

He rose slightly, found her lips and laved his attention on them just as he had her breasts. Raising his head, he grunted, "Take your clothes off, Hadleigh."

He didn't have to tell her twice. He reared back and pulled his shirt off with ease, then unbuckled his belt, unzipped and slid his pants and underwear down together and there he stood before her. Muscles rippling, tattoos every-where and impressively hard and erect for her. Wow! And then Wow! again.

She shimmied her pants over her hips and he reached forward and pulled them from her legs. She finished removing her blouse and bra as he climbed back up on the bed to her. He looked at the curls between her legs, then he spread her legs wider and leaned down and softly slid his tongue up the entire seam of her pussy. Her head dropped to the bed and her eyes closed as his tongue continued to part her lips and manipulate her body.

Her skin heated as he suckled on her clit; feelings and pleasures she'd never known engulfed her body as he expertly had her panting and moaning before the white-hot explosion of her orgasm washed over her. But he didn't stop.

His forefinger slowly slid inside of her then back out, and he repeated this as he sucked on her clit once again and she cried out, "Oh my God," as she came once again.

He crawled up her body then, rose up and quickly slid a condom on, which she'd not even seen him pull out of his pocket, then he dropped down to her, kissed her lips once again and murmured, "You're the most gorgeous woman I've ever met Hadleigh Watterson."

His tongue slid in her mouth at the same time he entered her body and it was incredible. His tongue mimicked his cock, in and out as he made love to her. Her legs had been limp noodles after two orgasms, but they were beginning to come to life once more as her tender tissues felt him push inside, and rub against her outside, his hips thrusting steadily, his muscles bunching and straightening under her hands as she roamed over his back while her mind tried absorbing all of it. Every. Second. Of. It.

He whispered, "Can you go again?" Then his lips kissed her ear.

"No, your turn."

She came to life for him. Her hips met his thrust for thrust; she wanted him to feel what she was feeling. She wanted him to remember this too, because she would. No one had ever felt like this. Had ever made love to her like this. Had ever made her body respond like this. No one. Ever.

His breathing increased and he groaned long and loud as his orgasm released. He pushed into her and held still as he spilled himself fully. Muscles spent, he lay on her more, holding himself up on his elbows and forearms, but his lips were next to her ear and his ragged breathing excited her.

After he caught his breath, he kissed the shell of her ear, then along her jaw, then her lips before he said, "Damn."

29

Van pushed his plate away and sighed. "That was fantastic Hadleigh. You're a great cook."

"Thank you. My mother taught me well. She insisted I know how to cook for myself so I could be self-sufficient."

"She did a great job."

"Let me clean up and we can sit in the living room."

Van stood. "Nope, we can clean up together, then sit in the living room."

Hadleigh smiled as she grabbed her empty plate and the bowl the carrots had been in; he picked up his plate and the meat platter with the bits of leftover roast on it. He followed her into the kitchen and set them on the counter, then quickly returned to the dining room to clean up more.

He carried the leftovers, salt and pepper shakers, and the empty wine glasses into the kitchen. Hadleigh smiled at him and carefully took the dishes from him and set them on the counter.

He held onto the wine glasses. "I'll refill these."

She giggled and he thought the pink in her cheeks was adorable. He poured them each more wine and he loaded the dishwasher while Hadleigh put away the remaining food.

After the counter was cleared, she wiped it off and turned to look at him. "I'm very sorry about everything this afternoon."

He let out a breath. "I understand Hadleigh. But you need to let me take care of this. We know what we're doing."

"I do know that. It's just that it takes so long and I can't help but wonder what's going on in that house during all this time."

"That's the hard part." He leaned against the counter behind him and crossed his arms. "You need to get that out of your head and focus on collecting all the evidence. I promise you it's so much worse if you don't have enough to actually convict these guys and they run. It's harder to catch them the next time and they rarely curb their activities. They make too much money off of it. As frustrating as it is, we have to do the due diligence."

"I understand. I do. I'll try harder to be patient as we wait."

He walked to her and wrapped his arms around her. He lay his head on top of hers and whispered, "We'll get him."

His heart picked up speed as her arms circled his waist and pulled him in tight. He then pulled away and looked Hadleigh in the eyes.

"I have Piper and Caiden, two of our cyber team, looking into Janine, your co-worker's runaway. We'll see if we can find anything on her, too. And, full disclosure, they're watching the profile you created to contact Marco48. It's necessary so our investigation isn't blown."

She bit her bottom lip and his body tingled. She clearly didn't know how sexy he thought that was.

"Okay. I won't contact him anymore. If he contacts me, I'll delete it."

"I appreciate that Hadleigh. I also know you're trying to help and I appreciate that too. There might be some things you can do to help us if you're interested."

She didn't hesitate and he smiled when she immediately responded, "Yes, I want to help."

He was about to answer when her phone rang.

"I'm sorry." She shrugged and picked up her phone which had been laying on the counter.

When she looked at the display her brow furrowed. "Hi Lucy, what's up?"

He watched as her face lost all its color and she fell back to lean against the counter behind her. Something was definitely wrong.

He waited through her conversation, only hearing her side which largely wasn't helpful at all. When she hung up, there were tears in her eyes and the look on her face worried him.

"That was my boss, Lucy. Autumn is missing."

"Autumn? The little girl the Connerts are fostering?"

"Yeah."

She started crying and he once again held her close and let her cry into his chest. He inhaled and exhaled deeply and slowly as she cried and his mind buzzed with questions, but he needed to let her get this out and then compose herself so he could ask them.

This wasn't good at all. Two girls missing in one week. Activity was ramping up.

Hadleigh pulled away and walked to the bathroom where he heard her blow her nose and wash her hands. When she came out of the bathroom, she feigned a smile; he walked to her, grabbed her hand, and led her to the sofa. Once they'd seated themselves, he twisted to look at her, but took her hand in his for the connection. He wanted to maintain the connection, but suspected that she needed it right now, too.

"When you're ready, can you tell me what you know?"

"Yes."

She inhaled and let it out in a whoosh, then lightly cleared her throat. "So, Lucy got a call from Bethany that Autumn hadn't returned from school today. She was back to in-person classes for the time being. She isn't sure where she went and has been out looking for her just recently. She was panicked and scared and didn't know what to do. She called the police and was told what they tell everyone, you have to wait twenty-four hours to ensure they are missing. And, just like Janine, it's sad because Autumn's a foster and her parents aren't really involved in her life, so there's no one to keep the pressure on and get the word out that these kids are missing."

"Did Bethany say if Autumn had plans after school? Did she belong to any activities, sports, art club, anything that might help find her?"

Hadleigh shook her head. "Lucy told me not to contact the Connerts. I'll look in Autumn's file when I get back to the office in the morning, but I don't recall that she'd joined anything. She was considering a couple after school activities but nothing that would keep her out this late."

Hadleigh looked at the clock on the bottom right corner of her television. It read 8:25 pm.

"Okay. I can do a couple of things." He pulled his phone from his back pocket and opened his messages. "I'll ask Piper and Caiden to view the footage from the cameras we have on the Connert house."

"You have cameras on the house?"

"Yes." He stopped texting and looked at her. The surprise on her face spoke volumes.

"You're surprised at this?"

"Of course, I am. I didn't know..." She stopped talking and looked into his eyes. "I guess it never occurred to me."

"We told you we were watching the house."

"Right, but I thought you meant, sitting in a car across the street watching, not cameras and stuff."

Then her eyes grew round. "Oh my God, you aren't bugging their house are you?"

"No, we aren't bugging the house. That's illegal."

"But a camera isn't?"

"No."

He finished his text to Piper then looked up at Hadleigh. "If you think of anything, let me know. Even if it seems small, I'd like to know. We'll begin doing some searches on the internet too. Do you happen to know if Autumn had a phone, a computer, or access to any of these at home? I assume at school she has a computer and we can have police do some digging on that. I also know the cops in town. I'll contact Rory Richards, the lead detective at Lynyrd Station PD and see if he'll do some work before the twenty-four-hour time is up."

"Wow, thank you so much."

Another tear fell and she quickly swiped it away. "I feel responsible in a weird way."

"You aren't, Hadleigh."

"I know, but if I had filed a report when I was suspicious, it may have made a difference."

He cupped the back of her head with his hand and she looked up at him. "We don't know that one thing has anything to do with the other. And, we don't know what that thing is. But this is a great time to do some information gathering. Will Lucy work with you on gathering it?"

"I don't know, but since it's escalated to this point, I sure hope so. Her mom is sick now too and she's preoccupied. The best thing right now is for her to tell the Connerts they have to work with me. But I don't know if she will."

"It's the best thing for us. Maybe not for the Connerts. All you can do is ask."

30

H adleigh was at the office early to speak with Lucy. She hadn't slept much last night anyway. It was a shame because Van spent the night with her and she had this big hunk in bed next to her but couldn't fully appreciate it because of her guilt over Autumn. Still, he held her until she fell asleep and she woke up with him spooning her, which was so sexy. She'd never had that in her life. All these firsts were racking up; she wanted to savor them, but all this other stuff kept getting in the way.

She nervously straightened her desk, organized her files for the day, then she went to fill her favorite cup with water all while nervously watching the door for Lucy.

Finally at ten minutes till eight she heard Lucy enter the office and her nerves hit overdrive in anticipation of their conversation.

Lucy stopped at the door to Hadleigh's office, "Let me get a cup of coffee and then come to my office Hadleigh, we'll chat."

"Okay." She swallowed the lump in her throat, stood, happy her knees were steady, and then made the short trek to Lucy's office. As a social services office, they were always short on space and their offices weren't spacious by any means. They were a low budget, no frills, and little amenities office. That meant their offices were all in a row with a narrow hallway on one end of the building, and two conference rooms and one room, where distraught children were cared for while waiting for placement, was at the front of the building. It was the only room that was brightly colored and somewhat happy.

She entered Lucy's office just as Lucy sat down behind her desk. Lucy looked up at her and shook her head. "Doesn't look like you slept much last night."

Hadleigh sat in the plastic chair across the desk.

"No, I didn't. How about you?"

"Nope. I haven't been getting much sleep these days."

"I'm sure you aren't."

Lucy opened a file on her desk. Hadleigh recognized it as her file on Autumn Lynn.

"I'll make this quick Hadleigh. Autumn did not come home from school yesterday and she did not come home last night. The Connerts spent a bit of time looking for her, but Bethany has Henry to take care of, so Melvyn looked around at places he knew she might have gone; with no luck. Luckily this morning, local police detective Rory Richards called me to inquire about what information I had on Autumn."

Hadleigh's heartbeat accelerated. Van had called Rory and asked him to begin his investigation. She was so grateful to him for this.

"That's wonderful."

"It is." Lucy continued in her no-nonsense way. "I told Bethany this morning that you are back on her case and we don't have anyone else, so she needed to get over it. My mother will likely not make the night and I have to be there with her. I want to be there with her."

Hadleigh shook her head. "I'm so sorry Lucy."

Lucy waved her hand as if to dismiss the comment, but Hadleigh knew she didn't want to break down crying, so she wasn't going to allow herself to step into the despair of her feelings right now.

"So." Lucy looked up at her, a sad smile on her lips. "Go to the Connerts this morning and get as much information as you can get about Autumn's last moments at home yesterday. Speak with Detective Richards first if you have to so you have what the Connerts' have already told him. It'll just frustrate them to have to repeat it all."

"I will. Thank you." Hadleigh stood. "Was everything alright at home with them yesterday? Did they have a disagreement with Autumn?"

"Bethany says no, it was a normal day. No warning signs. Nothing strange going on between them."

Hadleigh swallowed. "What about Bethany's brother. Did anything happen with him?"

Lucy closed the file on her desk and held it out to Hadleigh. "She said no one in the house had any type of disagreement or altercation with Autumn."

Hadleigh took the file and nodded. "Okay."

"Tread lightly with that line of questioning Hadleigh. It sets Bethany off like nothing else does."

Hadleigh took a deep breath. "I know it does and if there wasn't anything untoward going on, I don't know why a few innocent questions send her over the edge so quickly."

Lucy folded her hands together on her desktop and looked deeply into Hadleigh's eyes.

"We both feel that way, and I suspect you're correct on much of this Hadleigh. Now that police are involved, they'll do some hard digging. And I did mention to Bethany last night, as she was sniping at me for asking questions about Brent, that unless she didn't want any more children to be placed with her, she'd take this investigation seriously and not impede it in any way. For the most part it silenced her, but I suspect the fact that she felt you were snooping and getting close to something just may set her off once more. I'm just giving you fair warning."

Lucy's phone which was sitting on her desktop buzzed and she looked down at it. Then absently said, "It's the hospice care calling. I need to take this."

Hadleigh left Lucy's office and went back to hers to get her file bag and start her day. After she got into her car, she dialed Van's number.

"Good morning, beautiful."

Aww, she just melted a little bit. "Good morning, handsome."

"What's happening with Autumn?"

"Nothing. I've been told to go to the Connerts and get some more questions answered. Rory Richards is beginning his investigation. Thank you for calling him and asking him to get started on it."

Van chuckled on the other end of the phone and it made butterflies swarm in her tummy. "You're welcome sweetheart. I know you were worried and I know you didn't sleep well last night. But, when I pulled you close to me and wrapped my arms around you, you settled a bit."

Her brow furrowed. "Really?"

"Yep. You settled in and drifted off to sleep. I lay awake for a while listening to your steady breathing and thinking that holding you was a great way to spend my time."

She hesitated a moment, stunned at his comments. "That means you likely didn't get a lot of sleep. I'm sorry."

He chuckled again and she closed her eyes enjoying the sound of it. "I'm used to sleeping in spurts. If I'm on a mission it's how I rest. Don't worry about me."

"Okay." She swallowed and let the warm comfortable feelings wash over her. "Would you like to meet me at the Connerts'? We could tell them you're there to help me find Autumn. Maybe you'll see things I won't."

"I'll meet you there."

31

D onovan walked into the conference room and saw Piper and Caiden at their computers.

Piper looked up. "Hey Van. Charly went out to check a couple spots some runaways have been seen at lately. Caiden and I have the file for you."

She handed him a thick file.

Caiden turned to look at him. "In short, no, Brent Jennings did not borrow money from the Connerts or pay them any large sums recently. Also no on JenMark's assets. There was only around $10,000 of assets in the LLC. No other hidden sums of money or assets anywhere in either of the Connerts' names, or Brent Jennings. Jennings owns a home in California. A condo I think. He's not there much and it's only worth about half a million, which in California almost makes it barely livable." He smirked at his joke and Van couldn't help but chuckle. Everyone knew the high cost of living out there.

Piper shook her head. "I'm following up on anything the Connerts may have had a loan on and paid off recently, like another vehicle or home or something that would explain a bit of cash. I'm also running a search right now across the US for any other LLCs or corporations in which the Connerts are involved. It'll take a bit. But that could be why we can't find much in their names. The payments on their house are current, though JenMark LLC is the mortgagee on it. The Escalade was paid for in cash apparently; there are no loans for it."

"Thank you both for all your work on this. It helps us to know what direction not to look."

Van turned to leave and the door opened. Deacon Smythe, their third Team Cyber member and a former SEAL, entered the room. He walked with a limp as his right leg had been shattered in an IED explosion years prior. He joked that he had more metal in his body than a robot due to all the pins holding his leg together. It prohibited him from running or climbing, which was why he retrained for a cyber team. He had a real knack in cyber security though, so some things, no matter how awful, happen for a reason.

"Hey Deac, long time no see."

"Yeah. I was on a mission of sorts, training on some new software we're getting in that will give us more search options and has a far-reaching arm. It's epic for certain."

"That's cool. There'll be no stopping you guys now."

"Hey." Piper joked.

"You folks, I meant. Sorry Pipes."

Piper laughed and turned back to her computer. "Have a great day, Van. Go get that asshole."

Van nodded, socked Deacon in the upper arm and walked out of the conference room. He was eager to see Hadleigh; he was just as excited to gather more information so that hopefully, tomorrow night when he had his chance with Marco48, he'd be there with the cops and able to arrest him.

As he drove to the Connerts he saw a text come in from Charly. Pushing the connect button on his steering wheel he said, "Read text."

"Text from Charly. Autumn is not anywhere to be found."

He let out a deep sigh and wondered what this meant that two girls from the same small town were suddenly missing. Things hadn't escalated to this degree up until now. Not in this town anyway. But then again, a small town with a bunch of foster kids was like a sweet treat to a pedophile. Untapped potential for grooming and kidnapping. It was sickening.

He turned down the street the Connerts lived on and smiled when he saw Hadleigh's car sitting out front. He pulled in behind her car and smiled even bigger when he saw she was still sitting inside.

As he got out of his SUV she exited her vehicle and they met in the middle. He bent down and pulled her close and kissed her soft lips—onlookers be damned. She giggled as her arms wrapped around his shoulders and he thought nothing could be better than this feeling right here.

"I know it's only been a couple of hours, but I'm happy to see you."

The smile she bestowed on him was brilliant. "I'm happy to see you too."

He gave her another squeeze, then said, "Are you ready for this?"

"Yep, let's get it over with."

She reached into her car and pulled Autumn's file from inside the satchel. Then turned toward the house and he walked beside her. As they walked up the front steps, the door opened and Melvyn Connert stood in the doorway.

"Hi." he said sheepishly as he looked at Hadleigh.

Melvyn's head then turned toward him and cocked to the left a bit. He stared at Van for a few moments then finally said, "Didn't I see you at the Copper Cup the other night?"

"Yes, you did. I was there with Hadleigh."

Melvyn's brows furrowed as he looked again at Hadleigh, then his face cleared and he showed no emotion or recognition. Hadleigh spoke to him. "Mr. Connert, we're here to talk to you and Bethany about Autumn. May we come in?"

"Might as well, Detective Richards is here now, too."

Melvyn stepped back and allowed them into the living room. As they entered Rory stood and walked toward them. He held out his hand and shook Van's.

"Hi Van, nice to see you." He turned to her. "I presume you're Hadleigh Watterson."

"Yes. Nice to meet you, Detective."

"Good morning, Bethany. How are you holding up?" Hadleigh asked. Bethany looked like she'd been crying and hadn't slept much last night.

Bethany glanced up at Hadleigh from her seat in a recliner; her lips grew thin but she quietly said, "I'm about as well as can be expected."

Rory addressed Hadleigh and Van. "So Mr. and Mrs. Connert have told me that nothing unusual took place yesterday and that when Autumn left for school it was just like any normal day. She ate her usual breakfast, packed a lunch, and left with a wave saying she'd see them later. Just like she always does."

"Were you both home when she left for school?"

Melvyn nodded and Bethany looked at him but said nothing.

"How about Brent?"

Bethany's face changed as she glared at Hadleigh. "Don't you start with your suspicions, Hadleigh Watterson."

Rory stepped in, "Hold on. There's no accusation being made and we're all trying to accomplish the same thing in finding Autumn. Who's Brent?"

Bethany crossed her arms over her chest but said nothing. Hadleigh turned her head to look at Melvyn, who muttered, "He left yesterday."

32

Hadleigh turned her head to look at Van. She saw his jaw clench and release and knew this wasn't good news. They may have just let Marco48 slip away and take two girls with him.

Rory asked once again, "Who is Brent?"

Bethany and Melvyn both looked at their laps so it was left to her.

"Brent is Bethany's brother. He was here visiting and was supposed to stay three weeks."

Hadleigh looked at Bethany. "Bethany, why did he leave early? How can we get in touch with him?"

Bethany shook her head. "He said the studio he's working for called and wanted him to travel to a potential location."

"Do you know where that location is Bethany?"

Bethany looked her in the eye and some of the previous anger subsided, which Hadleigh was grateful for.

"I don't know where he is, where the location is, or anything else."

Rory Richards was writing in his notebook then looked up at Bethany. "I need his contact information Mrs. Connert. Phone number, address, email, and anything else you have. It is more to rule him out as a potential kidnapper than to accuse him. We have absolutely no proof of Brent being involved in anything but we do want to rule out any possible suspects."

"I'll get you what I have." Bethany mumbled and then stood from her chair hesitantly before walking toward the dining room and pulled her purse from the floor along-side the buffet standing at the far wall. Reaching inside she pulled her phone out and began scrolling through it. Rory Richards walked toward her and looked over her shoulder which irritated Bethany.

"Are you spying on me now?"

"No ma'am. But, until we are able to rule Brent out as a suspect, I don't want you sending him a text message to run or hide."

Bethany rolled her eyes then scrolled through her phone for Brent's contact information. She turned her phone and showed it to Rory, who wrote things down on his notebook. He then took Bethany's phone. "I'll hang on to this for the time being."

Bethany's lips thinned to a non-existent level and the anger in her eyes would have killed Rory if they could.

Melvyn then stood from his seated position, "Beth. Honey, come on in here."

Bethany ignored him as she glared at Rory.

"Beth, honey, please come in here." Melvyn repeated.

Bethany then turned let out a heavy sigh and slowly walked back to the living room and sat on the sofa beside Melvyn.

Rory caught Van's eyes with his. Something unspoken passed between them and she couldn't help but wonder what it was. Rory then went to the living room and took a seat on the love seat at a forty-five-degree angle to the sofa, where he'd been seated previously.

"How long did Brent stay here?"

Melvyn answered, "He was here just a few days."

"And his job asked him to leave to check out another location?"

"Yes."

"Do you know if Brent and Autumn spent any time together?"

Melvyn cleared his throat. "We had dinner together most nights. Beth..." He turned to look at Bethany and a small smile transformed his somber face into a friendlier visage. "Beth likes us to have dinner together. She said it's important for the kids to have that stability and normalcy and it's important for us all to chat at a common place on a regular basis."

Hadleigh's shoulders dropped. That was one of the things that Bethany did so well with the fosters she looked after. Kids thrived within her home. She was proud of that. But, right now, Hadleigh felt bad for having made Bethany feel like she'd been doing something wrong when she did work so hard to make a better life for these kids who didn't have one.

Guilt weighed heavy on her when Van leaned down and whispered, "What did you witness when you saw Brent and Autumn together?"

She turned and looked up at Van. His eyes were earnest as she stared into them and the color seemed to change from the beautiful blue to a deeper almost gray shade. His pupils were large and his left eye, which he was legally blind in, looked even larger.

"I saw her smile at him when he was talking to her."

"Didn't you say she was wearing lip gloss?"

Hadleigh blinked, he remembered that little tidbit. "Yes."

"Could he have been grooming her?"

Tears instantly sprung to her eyes and the weight of her realization that she should have done something sooner nearly caused her knees to buckle. She didn't do her job. She let Autumn down. How many others were there that she didn't see?

Van reached up and swiped a tear from her cheek then licked his lips, which she found sexy. "We'll talk about it later."

She swiped the dampness from her cheeks with her fingers and looked up to see Bethany staring at her. Hadleigh tried to smile but her lips quivered and she didn't want to show weakness so she inhaled deeply and held her breath for a moment before letting it out again.

She looked up at Van. "I'm going to step outside."

He nodded at her and she made her way to the door without a word to anyone.

Once she was outside, she pulled her phone from her purse and pulled up Marco48's last message. Nothing further from him, so they were still on for tonight.

Sending the text she walked down the steps on the front porch and to her car. Then she walked a bit further as nervous energy surged through her body. Maybe it was the wrong thing to do but she had failed over and over recently and she was going to try and make this right somehow. If Brent was Marco48 maybe he was still close. Maybe his job didn't contact him at all and he was close because traveling with an eight-year-old who wasn't yours was hard to do. Rory would likely have the airports watching for him at this point and Van and his team would be monitoring airports as well. That left Brent to hunker down until things loosened up. But, why? Why did he leave now unless he thought Hadleigh had caught on to something and got nervous.

That's when Hadleigh remembered Bethany carrying the sheet and maybe the camera out to the garage. Turning she started walking back to the house and more specifically, the garage. She'd see if she could get in there and look for the camera.

33

Van walked out of the house with Rory alongside him, but his eyes were searching for Hadleigh. He caught a glimpse of her near the garage and he yelled, "Hadleigh, no."

She stopped and turned to look at him, her face twisted in a combination of anger and frustration.

"That camera is in the garage."

"You know you can't break into that garage and if you do and we do find something, it can't be used as evidence."

"But, Van..."

Rory stepped off the porch. "Hadleigh, please don't do that. I can ask for a search warrant and we can sit and watch the house until it arrives but don't do anything to prevent us from using anything we find as evidence."

She let out a deep breath as her shoulders sank down.

Van's phone alerted him to a text and he pulled his phone from his pocket and looked at the text from Piper.

"Hadleigh just made contact with Marco48 asking to meet him tonight."

His lips thinned as he read the text and his neck tightened to the point of pain. Slowly, he looked up at Hadleigh as he took steps toward her. "Did you make contact with Marco48?"

A flurry of emotions washed across her face. Her mouth opened then closed and he continued walking toward her. "Please tell me you didn't."

"I screwed up. I let Autumn down. I have to fix it."

"You're going to fuck the whole thing up. Not fix it. He'll get away for certain."

"Not if I'm there." She looked past him to Rory who stood watching them. "Rory, can you be there too, just in case?"

Rory looked between them, first at Van then at Hadleigh and so many things showed on his face. "I don't want to get in the middle of this, you two."

"You're not. But, if I can make contact with Brent, would you be there to arrest him?"

Van turned to Rory then, "Let's go talk about what we can do."

Rory nodded. "Come to the station and we'll talk there."

Van nodded, then turned and put his arm around Hadleigh's shoulders. Though he wanted to throttle her but good, he also wanted to keep her where he could watch her.

"You'll ride with me."

"I can't leave my car here."

"Yes, you can and you will."

"Van, this is bullshit. I'm not a child."

"Then stop acting like one."

She stopped and he nearly fell over at her sudden halt. He turned to look at her.

"I've asked you not to make contact and you promised."

"I don't think I actually promised."

"You promised, Hadleigh."

"I actually promised I wouldn't meet with him last night. And I didn't, in case you don't remember. But that was before Autumn went missing and tonight could be a chance to get him and keep him from leaving town with Autumn."

He clenched his jaw so tightly he thought he'd break his teeth as he stared at this beautiful woman he was falling for and she was once again betraying his request to not get involved to a level that she fucked up his investigation.

"What's going on here?"

Van heard Charly as her heels clicked along the cement driveway they all stood on now.

"Hadleigh made contact with Marco48 asking him to meet tonight."

Charly stopped in front of them and looked at Hadleigh. A soft smile appeared on her face as she said, "I know. I got the text too."

Hadleigh crossed her arms in front of her. "How do you know that I contacted him, anyway?"

Van looked Hadleigh in the eyes. "We're logged on and watching his email and texts."

"That's...Isn't that illegal?"

Van shrugged and Charly added. "We aren't cops. We do what we need to do to stop pedophiles and perverts. If it means crossing the proverbial lines here and there, I don't feel bad about that. We don't have to follow the same rules law enforcement has to follow." Charly then tilted her head and looked at Rory. "No offense Rory."

Rory shook his head and raised his hands in the air. "None taken. Basically, we're all trying to accomplish the same thing."

Van looked at Charly, "We're headed to the police department to discuss where we go from here. Rory has Brent's phone number and contact information; I'll send it all over to Piper so Cyber can begin running Brent down. Hopefully he hasn't turned off the tracking on his cell phone and we can still find him."

Then a light switched on and he looked at Hadleigh. "Does Autumn have a phone? Computer? Even if it's one she uses at school. She's missing so we can use that as evidence."

He turned to Rory. "Can you get a search warrant for that?"

Rory nodded and pulled out his phone as he stepped a few feet away. Maybe they'd find out who Autumn was touching base with and hopefully it will lead us somewhere.

Van's phone chimed again, and so did Charly's. Taking a deep breath, he pulled his phone up and read the screen.

"For fuck's sake, what the hell?" He muttered.

Hadleigh lay her hand on his arm. "What is it, Van?"

"Another runaway in town. A ten-year-old boy named Miguel. Went missing last night."

Hadleigh visibly swallowed and her eyes gathered moisture. "Is he also a foster?"

Van shrugged. "I don't know yet."

He typed the question into his phone and took Hadleigh's hand in his. "Let's go to the station and discuss what we can do from here."

He looked at Charly, "Are you coming with us Charly?"

She smiled and shook her head. "Nope, it looks like you've got it covered. I'm going to sit across the street with a cup of coffee and watch the house here. While I'm doing that, I'm going to do some searching on my laptop for Marco48's online activity in the past day and see if I can get the IP address from Piper or Caiden on where the last couple of texts came from."

Charly looked at Hadleigh, "Did Marco48 respond to your request to meet tonight?"

Hadleigh shook her head slowly, "No. Not yet."

"Do me a favor Hadleigh, let me know if he does. Maybe I'll meet with him and have Emmy or Falcon come with me to apprehend him. We'll call PD if we are able to get him."

Hadleigh nodded. "I will. Do you know where Miguel disappeared from?"

34

S itting in Rory Richard's office, Hadleigh remained quiet. Not that she had to, but she wanted to learn so she didn't mess up this investigation. She liked what Van and his colleagues were doing and she wanted to know more. Listening to Van and Rory talk, she learned so much that she didn't know about the law and also about runaways in general. As a social worker, she had always felt armed with knowledge on runaway behavior, but listening to these two, she realized she had so much yet to learn. Miguel's last sighting hadn't been uncovered yet.

Van turned his head toward her and smiled, "You're very quiet."

"I'm learning."

He smiled and she enjoyed seeing this, Van. The one who wasn't mad at her. The other Van was a little intimidating.

He leaned forward toward Rory and said, "So, we're waiting for a search warrant for the garage. We're hoping to find the camera. Charly's watching to make sure no one goes out to the garage so we'll know if they try to move it. We're also waiting for a search warrant for Autumn's computer at school. Can you also see about Miguel and Janine's computers? Maybe we can link those three together."

"Yep, I've got a team member working on those as well. Judge Mackintosh is on the bench today and is usually fairly accommodating if we have some solid reasoning behind needing the warrant. Three missing kids is pretty compelling."

"Roger that."

Van stood then and reached across Rory's desk and shook his hand. "Thanks for your assistance on this Rory."

"We want these scumbags off the streets as much as you do."

Van turned to her and held out his hand. "Are you ready Hadleigh?"

Nodding she stood. "Yeah." She looked at Rory, "Thank you for including me in all of this. It helps to have the legal information so I can help and not hinder you all."

Rory smiled at her and she realized what a handsome man he was. The photographs on his desk of him and a gorgeous redhead told the story of a happy man and she was thrilled for him.

"We appreciate that Hadleigh."

Van opened the door and waited for her to pass through before following her. She purposely brushed past him closer than she needed, because she wanted to. She heard his intake of breath and she smiled. The seriousness of the situation was disheartening, but she felt this new-found love in her whole body and it was exciting. She stumbled a bit as the realization of her thoughts flooded her. Love? Love? That seemed rather impossible so soon. They'd only had one date. Well, two, but still.

"Okay Hadleigh, I just got a text from Piper. Miguel's last name is Gonzales. Do you know him from any of your foster files? We're running some searches on him right now. Piper is on the phone with the principal of the school. All the kids are enrolled at Lynyrd Station Middle school."

"I don't recognize his name. I've not come across it in any of my files."

Van typed something into his phone, then took her hand and led her from the police station to his SUV.

Once he'd climbed into his vehicle, he started it up, then turned to her and smiled. "I've got to go to the school and see if the principal will let me see the kids' computers. Rory's teammate got the search warrant. I just want to get the IP addresses to Piper and Caiden so they can search the computers before they head off to the police department."

"Is that legal?"

He merely looked at her, conflict written all over his face.

"Never mind, Van."

Here she was trying to learn the laws and some procedural things and Van was doing things completely outside the lines of the law. It boggled her mind, and yet Rory knew what they were doing was likely outside the law and acknowledged it and then moved on.

Van drove in silence for a few blocks and finally broke the silence. "You know when we have to step outside the lines it's because we're trying to save the kids. We'll do what it takes. Someday, remind me to tell you about how RAPTOR started. We all stepped way outside the lines and quit our jobs at the same time."

"You quit your..." She watched the beautiful smile on his face. He had the smallest dimple in his cheeks. How had she not noticed that before?

"It was fucking beautiful."

"What was?"

"Quitting. We all quit at the same time. Emmy, Charly, Diego, Caiden, and me."

"Oh, wow. I didn't know you all worked together prior."

"We did. We trained together and worked together. And that day, we saved three kids together."

"Wow. You're heroes."

His cheeks flushed pink at her compliment. The more she learned about him the more she liked him. All his co-workers, too. And she felt terribly insufficient in her work. She slogged through files and home visits and tried hard to place kids with families that would care for them, but then things happened. This whole situation had shaken her confidence in herself and the whole system now. I mean, really, what were they doing anyway?

Van pulled into the school parking lot and got out of the car. He walked around and opened her door, ever the gentleman, and took her hand as she stepped out of his vehicle. He then steered her to the front entrance of the school while saying, "Any word from Marco48?"

It took her out of her dreamy state in a heartbeat, but it didn't change how she felt about him. "No. Do you think he's gone?"

He shook his head. "Hopefully we'll find out from these computers. Or, Cyber will find information that will help us."

"I hope so, too."

"When we're finished here, I'd like you to go back to your office and get some information for me. The other girl, Janine, where was she staying? Get that address. Search for Miguel in the records, see if he's a foster. Then, get the names and contact information on any of the young girls who used to be fostered by the Connerts. Maybe we can find out some information from them on the goings on in the house."

"Oh my God, why didn't I think of that?"

Van shook his head, "Two heads are always better than one, Hadleigh. I didn't think of it right away either."

35

V an walked into the Neighborhood Cafe and saw Charly sitting at the table in front of the window. She looked up from her computer and smiled at him.

"Hey, how did it go?"

"Pretty good. Cyber is running the IPs on all three kids' computers as we speak. What have you seen here?"

"Nothing. I wonder if they suspect we're watching?"

Van shrugged. "Could be."

"Well, I've found something interesting and I just sent it over to Rory and Cyber team to confirm."

Van pulled out a stool at the bar height table and looked over at Charly's computer.

"Remember this guy?"

He watched as Charly played the video footage of the young boy who'd walked up to the Connerts' house when

Hadleigh was there, and he'd been there again later in the day.

"I'm wondering if this is Miguel," she pondered.

Van watched as Charly replayed the video for him.

"He looks to be around nine or ten."

"Right. But look how he's dressed. New shoes, nice clothes, his hair is neatly trimmed. Not that all fosters look like ragamuffins, but most of them don't have brand new shoes and most of them don't get regular haircuts. It's a luxury that not all foster families support. Sadly. And, if they do, it would likely be at the beginning of the month when they get paid. This boy has a fresh haircut."

"Great observations, Charly."

Charly smiled but kept watching the video.

"Yes and no. If that is Miguel and he isn't a foster, did he run away or was he abducted?"

Van squeezed his fists and cracked the knuckles on each hand as he let thoughts roll around his mind.

"I recall seeing him that night we met Hadleigh. He was just leaving the Connerts when we arrived. He walked down the street that way." He pointed down the street. "Then turned left at the end. Maybe I should take a walk and see if there is anyone looking for him somewhere down in that neighborhood. Maybe there will be posters somewhere."

"Good thinking."

Van got up and left the coffee shop. As he walked down the street his phone rang. "Keach."

Hadleigh giggled on the other end of the phone. "Watterson."

Van chuckled. "Sorry, I didn't look at my phone before I answered. Nice to hear from you."

"I found information on three young girls that have stayed with the Connerts in the past. One of them is now twenty-one. She was with them ten years ago and the first girl to foster at the Connerts. Not sure she'll be able to offer any assistance, but we could at least talk to her. The second one is nineteen now and she's in college at Valparaiso. The third one is eighteen and is still in town but leaving for college in the morning. I called her first and she said she'd meet with me this afternoon. I'm going over there in a couple of hours. Do you want to join me?"

"Yes, as a matter of fact I do. I'm just walking the neighborhood now where we watched that young boy leaving the Connerts' walk the other day. We have a hunch that might be Miguel."

"I was wondering about that too. Did Rory get back to you on his information?"

"Only that his last name is Gonzales. The school wouldn't allow me any other information on his family so we're doing our own investigation. Out of curiosity, would any of the girls you spoke to know Autumn? Do they stay in contact with the Connerts in any way?"

"I didn't ask. I was afraid to put them off before actually getting to meet with them. I thought I'd ask when I am able to sit with them face to face."

Van turned the corner and rubbed the back of his neck. "Good point. I'll see you in a little while. Where would you like me to meet you?"

"Why don't you come to my house. I came home to grab lunch before heading out this afternoon."

"Sounds good. See you in a few minutes."

Ending the call, Van came up to another street. He wasn't sure if he should turn down the street or keep going straight, so he decided to turn down the street, which would also run him behind the Connert house. Maybe he'd see something along the way that could help. The street was fairly empty as he walked. He worried he'd stand out since there wasn't anyone else walking today, but decided his best bet would be to walk the length of the street as if he'd intended to.

As he neared the back of the Connerts' home, he started looking into the yard, by the garage, and alongside the house in case someone was moving things around. If so, he'd call Charly and she could be watchful of anything on her side of the house. But the closer he got, the more he realized it was eerily quiet at the Connerts' home. Pushing off the uncomfortable feeling that he was being watched, he kept walking till he reached the first intersection. Deciding to walk back to his vehicle, he made another left and walked toward First Street.

Just as he neared the intersection of this street, which was Division Street, and First Street, Rory's car drove past. He must be heading to the Connerts' home and Van's heart beat a bit faster thinking Rory had gotten a search warrant. Van picked up his pace and began jogging to First Street. There he jogged past the few houses until he neared the Connerts'. Rory's car was parked on the street in front of their house.

He turned and looked toward the Neighborhood Cafe and saw Charly walking out the door. She caught his gaze and walked across the street to meet him.

As they got close enough to talk he asked, "Did you hear anything?"

"No, I just saw Rory pull in."

Both of their phones buzzed and they each looked down at their screens.

"Emmy sent an update."

"Rory received a search warrant for Brent's room at the Connerts'. Police in California are also going to his residence there."

A car pulled up to the curb and Detective Sam Bowers stepped from his vehicle. Charly sighed.

"You're practically drooling Charly," Van teased.

"My God, how can you not be?"

"Ah, he's not my cup of tea I guess."

"He's mine. He's my whole pot of tea."

Detective Sam Bowers was well known in Lynyrd Station. The women all swooned and he could always get a female suspect to tell him everything she knew about anything.

He wasn't cocky or arrogant, but he was huge at six foot eight inches and solid muscle. Van had been introduced to him when he first moved to Lynyrd Station and had to stop at the police department to work with Rory on his first case for RAPTOR. Sam towered over most everyone, yet he was a nice guy. He was divorced and likely the most eligible bachelor in town with an adorable seven-year-old daughter.

"Hey Van, what brings you here?"

"Same as you I'd guess. We've been working on a pedophile who's been soliciting young girls and boys to take nudes of them. Then he sells them to sickos. The IP we have is from this house. But, we're still gathering intel to make the case stick."

"Okay. We're searching the house for information leading to the missing girl who is living here, Autumn Lynn. Do you think the IP is linked to Mrs. Connerts' brother, Brent Jennings?"

"Right now, it sure looks that way. But I hate to say so definitively. I don't want to overlook other information."

Sam wrote something down on a small notebook he'd pulled from his back pocket. Tucking the notebook back into its pocket, Charly nearly sighed again as Sam's shirt stretched across his chest. Sam must have heard the sound that squeaked out of Charly's throat because his cheeks turned a bit red. He smiled at Charly then and Van thought she was going to fall to the ground at his feet. Sam headed up the walkway to the house. "Come to the station in a couple of hours and we'll be able to share what we've found so you can compare your notes with ours."

"Thanks, Sam. Will do." Van chuckled at Charly's wide-eyed nod to the detective.

Sam disappeared through the door of the house and Charly leveled a glare at him. "What?" she demanded.

He continued laughing as he walked to his car. "Obvious. I'm just saying, totally obvious."

36

Hadleigh put away her clean dishes from the dishwasher and straightened up her kitchen. A quick look at the clock told her Van should be here soon.

She was about to walk to the bathroom to brush her teeth when she heard his car pull into her driveway. Changing her direction, she opened the front door and smiled as he got out of his vehicle and walked toward her. She still got those little butterflies in her tummy when she saw him and she hoped they'd never go away.

Just as he reached the door her phone rang and she motioned with her hand to her phone on the counter and he nodded and let himself in.

Hadleigh glanced at her screen. "Hi Lucy."

"Hi Hadleigh. I'm afraid I'm calling with some bad news. I had a meeting with the district manager today and mentioned your suspicion that there was something going on in the Connerts' home. She informed me that you should have written the report and filed it. That's not to say Autumn would still be here or that you are at fault, but I'm afraid she's sending this one up the ladder to the state level and there may be some disciplinary action. I'm so sorry, Hadleigh."

"But you didn't think I needed to write the report. Not until I had better information."

"I'm aware and you're right, I erred on the side of getting more information and I shouldn't have. The disciplinary action may also hit me as well."

"What does that mean? Is it possible I could be fired?"

Lucy was quiet for some time. "I don't know, Hadleigh."

Hadleigh turned and saw Van watching her from across the room. His jaw was tight, his thumbs in his pockets as he leaned against the wall. He looked casual, but she could tell he wasn't. She took a deep breath and let it out, though it was shaky. Her knees trembled and she worried she'd fall down if she tried to walk. She'd never been fired before. She'd never done anything to cause her to be disciplined. Lucy had told her to get more information and she was trying to do that.

"Okay. Do you know when a decision will be made?"

"Likely a week, maybe two. Things don't move that fast at the state level."

"Right." Taking a deep breath to calm herself she softly replied again. "Right."

Lucy cleared her throat on the other end of the line, "One last thing, I'm afraid you're on unpaid leave until the decision is made, Hadleigh."

"What?"

Now her legs were shaking and she worried she'd break down any minute.

"Again, it seems all I can say is I'm sorry."

Hadleigh was unable to form words. Her vision grayed, and for a fleeting moment, she worried that her mind couldn't focus on any one thing.

"Okay," she replied to Lucy and slowly pulled her phone from her ear and tapped the end-call icon. Gently setting her phone on the counter she turned to look at Van, who still stood against the wall trying to look casual.

He pushed himself from the wall with a small movement from his shoulder and walked toward her.

He reached forward and pulled her into his body, his strong arms circled her waist and shoulders, his warm solid chest the perfect place to find comfort and safety. At this moment, she needed safety over everything else.

After long moments, he inhaled deeply, his lips on the top of her head placed soothing kisses, then his solid deep voice whispered, "This is exactly why I joined RAPTOR. No arbitrary rules. No red tape. No bullshit from the very people who should appreciate there are people like you willing to do the job you do. It's thankless all the way around. The powers that be work harder to push people into the little boxes they want you to stay in than they do performing the jobs they should be doing. In this case, making sure children are in solid, strong, healthy homes. Instead, they've tied your hands at every turn."

She sniffed and though she hoped it was somewhat lady-like, in her little cocoon in his arms, it sounded like a bull horn. She nodded her head and practiced some even breathing so she didn't break down and cry.

Van's strong hold relaxed and she looked up into his eyes. His beautiful, sincere, sexy eyes.

"So, I'm not sure if I can speak with Jenn Owens now, since I'm officially suspended."

Van stepped back and looked her in the eye. A soft smile creased his face, and it made him even more handsome if that was possible. "Now you're not working, you're helping to find out what is going on in the Connerts' home and you don't have to worry about stepping outside the lines."

"But if upper management finds out, I could actually get fired."

"Fuck them. I mean it, fuck them. Shouldn't they be more worried about three missing kids than whether or not you should have filed a fucking report?"

Hadleigh straightened her spine. "They should be."

"Exactly. Bureaucracy is the death of so many things. Let's work together on this mission along with Charly and Piper and the others and then we'll figure things out for you."

She swallowed, "Why not? You're right, finding these kids and stopping Marco48 and people like him is so much more important. If I have to go work at a restaurant slinging food, I can do that."

His smile broadened and her heartbeat raced. God he was the best man she'd ever met.

He leaned down and kissed her lips, softly, sweetly molding perfectly to hers. Then, the mood changed. The heat rose and the intensity in both of their bodies erupted into something so much more. He unbuttoned and unzipped her slacks then his hands dove into them as they dropped to the floor, his hands then kneaded the flesh of her ass and pulled her into his hardness.

37

She smelled like all things good. A fresh summer breeze, clean linens in the summer, a hint of citrus and maybe honey. All of it combined into what he was now recognizing as Hadleigh Watterson. And, dammit, he'd fallen for her in a nano-second. He couldn't help it, she was...everything.

His hands roved over her body as she stood before him, naked now that she'd removed her blouse. She'd pulled off his shirt just a moment ago and was working on his zipper right this minute. His cock throbbed as the blood rushed to it, the tight confinement of his jeans making it painful. The instant Hadleigh had pushed his jeans and underwear over his hips, it sprang forward toward her, seeking her naturally.

She dropped to her knees and in one swift motion, had him in her mouth. "Fuck," he mumbled as he rested his hand on her head.

Her right hand slid down his leg, urging him to step from his jeans as her left hand held his cock to her mouth, her tongue wetting it from tip to base. He managed to step from one leg of his jeans then he lifted his other foot and allowed the jeans to slide off his foot as he sent them across the room. Spreading his legs apart so he was lower, he bent his knees slightly while Hadleigh worked him like a favorite violin. Up and down, sucking at the end, then quickly swallowing him up again. Fucking perfection. They found a rhythm, the two of them together, so much so that she let go of his cock, her nails dug into him as she grabbed the flesh of his ass with both hands, pushing him into her mouth.

He dug his hands into her hair and pulled it back so he could watch her as she sucked him off. The sight of her mouth on his cock, glistening from her saliva, made him harder if that were possible. Holding her head in place by her hair excited him like he'd never felt before. Catching a glimpse of her breasts swaying as she moved, his cock pushing in once more, her nails biting into his ass, it was more than he could take. His balls drew up painfully into his body and he came with the force of a volcano erupting.

To his surprise, she swallowed while he was fully inside of her and the movement of her throat on his cock sent shivers down his spine. Hadleigh sucked one last time and slowly let him fall from her mouth. She started to stand, her tongue swiping her lips as she did, but he halted her progress and instead lowered her to the plush rug on top of the hardwood floors in her living room.

He kissed her lips, softly and seductively, then kissed his way down her body, paying attention to each of her delicious breasts, sucking her nipples into his mouth and enjoying the arch of her back as he nibbled on the tips. He positioned himself between her legs, but continued kissing down her body until he felt the curly hairs tickle his lips. Teasing her, he kissed all around them, over one thigh and up again to the other. She pushed on his head and he smiled and continued to tease her.

She groaned a bit and he decided to make her feel as good as she'd made him feel. He kissed her to the separation in her lips, then swiped his tongue up the seam, opening her to him. She moaned as his tongue easily found her clit and swirled around a few times. Her hips arched and he sucked her clit into his mouth; she quivered. Repeating that movement, he reveled as her body ignited under his.

Inserting two fingers into her pussy he growled as Hadleigh moved under him. His fingers moved in and out as his tongue and lips continued to suck and lick her clit. Her hands grabbed at his hair as she fought for her orgasm.

Hadleigh raised her hips once more and moaned as her orgasm ran through her. Van stopped and watched her face as she came. He'd never tire of watching this beautiful woman as she came and he loved knowing he was the one giving her pleasure. Un-fucking-real.

Van crawled up Hadleigh's body, brushing light kisses across her flesh, watching the goose bumps form as he moved up to her neck.

"You are beautiful inside and out Hadleigh Watterson. That was fantastic."

Hadleigh wrapped her arms around his shoulders and whispered in his ear, "You are handsome inside and out Donovan Keach."

He maneuvered to the side and lay next to her, his mind reeling from these new feelings that had taken up residence in his body and not sure what to do about them. He'd never allowed himself to fall in love before and while he'd had girlfriends over the years, he'd never had feelings like these. Maybe he'd finally matured. Maybe Hadleigh was the one and she's what he'd been waiting for. Whatever the reason, he closed his eyes and enjoyed feeling complete for the first time in his life.

He inhaled a deep breath and let it out when Hadleigh turned to her side and laid her arm across his belly, head resting on his arm. His nipples pebbled as her sighing breath blew across them. Van squeezed her to him and kissed her head. This was...bliss.

38

Hadleigh pulled her hair back and tied it in a ponytail at the top back of her head. Freshly showered, she felt confident that she was doing the right thing, thanks to Van and his reassurances. They'd go and speak with Jenn Owens and with a little more luck on their side, they'd also be able to speak with one or both of the other girls Hadleigh had been able to locate.

She walked out of the bathroom, and smiled as she saw Van standing at the kitchen counter, finishing the lunch she'd saved for him.

"You could have taken a seat at the table or on the sofa."

He shrugged. "No need. I'm used to eating on the go."

She hugged him from behind and enjoyed the feel of his muscles under her fingers as she ran them up his torso.

"We're not really on the go."

"We will be in a few minutes."

She giggled and let him go. She leaned against the counter and watched him pop the last bite of the roast beef sandwich she'd made into his mouth. He licked his fingers and her body remembered his tongue as he brought her to orgasm; her nipples pebbled at the thought.

Her phone buzzed and she pulled it from her pocket. Standing up straight she looked at Van.

"Leslie Knot will also meet with us. She's another of the fosters. She's in college at Valparaiso but said if we can get there, she'll talk to us. Do you want to go on a road trip?"

"Sure. Why don't we drive over after we speak with Jenn? We can spend the night in a hotel, get up early, have breakfast and meet with Leslie."

Hadleigh excitedly typed out her message to Leslie and stared at her phone waiting for the reply. Finally, after a few moments, she replied, "Okay."

"She'll meet us tomorrow." She swallowed the nervousness that crawled up her throat.

"That's a good thing Hadleigh. If these girls had a great experience at the Connerts', we'll have to keep looking. But if they can shed any light on anything nefarious going on over there, we'll have something to go on."

"I know. I guess one part of me hopes these young ladies didn't have to suffer any horrible circumstances but I also want to catch this bastard and if they know anything at all, I'm hopeful they are strong enough to tell us."

Van nodded, put his plate in the dishwasher then looked at his watch. "Ready?"

"Yeah."

Hadleigh picked up her purse from the floor alongside the counter, tucked her phone in the side and headed for the front door.

As they climbed in Van's SUV, he pushed the Bluetooth button on his steering wheel. "Call Headquarters."

"Calling headquarters." The robotic voice repeated.

"Dillon."

"Hey Pipes, Hadleigh and I are on our way to interview two girls that used to live with the Connerts. One is in Valparaiso, so I won't be back until tomorrow. Any information from the kids' computers?"

"Yep. I was just about to call you actually. We found a couple of phone numbers on Autumn's computer. I've called the number and it appears Autumn has a secret phone. A young girl answered the phone and when I asked for Autumn, she asked who I was and I told her I was a friend looking for her. She hung up."

"Do you think it was Autumn?"

"I do. For what it's worth, she sounded fine and I'm running a trace on it now. Hopefully she won't turn it off or turn off the GPS."

"Okay. Keep me in the loop. Anything from Miguel or Janine?"

"Still running diagnostics on it."

"Thanks Pipes. What about Brent?"

"Still nothing on Brent. Also, Charly just texted and said Bethany Connert has gone out to her garage and hasn't come out in a while."

He turned and looked at her and she shook her head slowly. She just knew that camera was out there. She was likely destroying the evidence.

"Thanks Pipes."

Hadleigh's phone buzzed and she looked at the text that came through.

It was from Marco48. "How about we meet tonight at nine?"

She turned to Van. "Marco48 wants to meet me tonight."

Van's jaw tightened. "Ask him where."

Her fingers shook as she typed out "Where?"

She set her phone on her lap and stared out the window. Van kept driving and she tried pushing back the fear that occupied her emotions when it came to Marco48.

Her phone buzzed and she swallowed before looking down at it.

He'd responded. She picked up her phone and tapped the text to open it.

"Meet me at the Neighborhood Cafe."

She looked at Van, "He wants to meet at the Neighborhood Cafe. Isn't that a bit bold?"

"It sure is. Not only is he still around, he's still in the general area."

Van continued driving but she could tell he was thinking about this. Finally, he glanced over at her briefly before watching the road once again.

"Tell him you'll be there."

"But what about Valparaiso?"

"We're still going. Charly can meet him and haul his ass in."

"If you have him then why would we still go to meet with Leslie?"

Van cleared his throat. "We still need the evidence. We still need to know what's been going on in that house. We may have to ask Leslie to testify in court if need be."

Hadleigh swallowed and stared out the windshield. This all just made her a bit nervous. She hadn't mentioned anything to Leslie about the possibility of having to go to court. She didn't even know if she was still employed and if reaching out to former fosters was appropriate. But she did know that Van was right. They did need to know what was going on in that house.

Before she responded to Marco48 she turned in her seat to face Van.

"I really want to be there when they arrest Brent Jennings. Can we be there? We can drive through the night to Valparaiso, I'll drive."

His eyes met hers for a moment before he nodded. "Yes, we can make that happen."

She sighed in relief as she texted Marco48. "I'll be there at nine."

39

H e pulled his SUV into the driveway of the home where Jenn Owens was living. The house was a nice white ranch-style home on the outskirts of Lynyrd Station. The landscaping was neat and healthy, the lawn mowed with the stripes running at an angle. The driveway was black topped and there was an extra-large yard off to the left of the driveway which had a wooden swing set and an extra three-stall garage. It looked like a nice happy home.

"What do I need to know about Jenn Owens?" he asked Hadleigh.

"She's eighteen. She lived with the Connerts four years ago for eight months. When she left it was at her request. She didn't complain much about the Connerts, just that she had met Mrs. Janssen, whose house we're at now, in school. Mrs. Janssen is also a volunteer at the school and she and Jenn developed a relationship. Mrs. Janssen then applied to be a foster, had her house inspected and went through all the proper channels to accept fosters. Jenn is the only foster she's ever had to the best of my knowledge. This isn't my home responsibility. Mrs. Janssen has three biological children who are all grown and now out of the house."

"Was Jenn in trouble or did she have any problems that you're aware of?"

Hadleigh shook her head and he couldn't help but notice little things he loved such as that her lips were full and soft and he enjoyed kissing them. Her eyes were the prettiest brown he'd ever seen. The way the sun glimmered in them made her look unearthly. Her hair shone with golds and reds and coppers where the sun touched it and he enjoyed all of those colors. He was a totally lost man. She had taken him by the balls and wrapped him up tightly. But he liked that he felt that way.

"No, she wasn't at all."

"Okay, shall we go in?"

Van got out of the SUV and walked around the front of it to open Hadleigh's door. Once he did, he reached his hand in to help her out and he enjoyed the sparks that ignited when they touched. He'd much rather be spending his time tonight making love to her in a hotel than driving through the night, but he was also eager to get this bastard and the sooner they did, the sooner they would be able to begin their lives together.

Before they reached the door, it opened and a kind looking older woman smiled at them from the entry.

"Hello and welcome to our home."

Hadleigh smiled at the woman. "Thank you, Mrs. Janssen, we appreciate your hospitality."

"Of course, anything to help."

Van held his hand out to Mrs. Janssen and she met his gaze as she shook his hand.

"My name is Donovan Keach, Mrs. Janssen."

"Nice to meet you Mr. Keach."

He nodded and smiled, "Donovan or Van is fine."

She led them through the living room and into the dining room where a young girl sat at the table. As they entered the room she stood and when her eyes landed on Hadleigh, she swallowed what seemed like a large lump in her throat.

"Hi Jenn, thank you so much for meeting with me."

"Sure." Jenn then looked up at him and he saw her lips quiver in nervousness.

"I'm Donovan, a friend of Hadleigh's. I came with her because we're both working on a case that we're hoping you can help us with."

Jenn's hands folded together and clenched and he could tell this was a nervous young lady. Why would she be so nervous?

Mrs. Janssen stepped forward. "Please sit down. Can I get you something to drink? Water? Tea? Coffee? A soda perhaps?"

He shook his head and Hadleigh smiled at Mrs. Janssen. "No, thank you, Mrs. Janssen."

They took seats at the table, he and Hadleigh on one side, Mrs. Janssen directly across from him and Jenn directly across from Hadleigh.

Hadleigh folded her hands on top of the table and looked at Jenn directly. "Jenn, I'm so happy and proud of you for going off to college. You should be proud of yourself for your accomplishment."

Jenn turned and looked at Mrs. Janssen. "It's because of Mom. She's the best thing that ever happened to me."

Mrs. Janssen teared up and took Jenn's hands in hers. "You're the best thing to ever happen to Frank and me, Jenn. We love you."

Jenn leaned over and kissed Mrs. Janssen on the cheek then turned back to Hadleigh. "So many kids in the system don't have good families who will teach them not only how to live on their own once they're out, but also make them feel like a part of the family. Before coming here, I'd been in seven foster homes. Most thought of me as a number and that number was the amount of money they were getting from the state for having me in their home. Most of the other kids steal from each other, lash out against each other, and are generally all lost souls. I felt that way, too. Then I met Mom at school and she showed me love. And to value myself, and that I was important. The happiest day of my life was moving in here."

Mrs. Janssen pulled a tissue from her pocket and wiped her eyes. She then looked at Hadleigh, "I saw Jenn needed love. She needed to feel valued and that she mattered. My heart reached out to hers and her heart embraced mine. It was meant to be."

Hadleigh sniffed beside him and Van blinked rapidly to keep himself from tearing up.

Clearing his throat lightly, he asked, "Jenn, the reason we're here is that we want to ask you about your time at the Connerts'. Can you tell us what life was like living with them?"

40

Jenn smiled at Van before she responded to his question. Her eyes darted to his arms and lingered on the tattoos there before looking into his eyes again.

"It was alright there. Mrs. Connert is a good cook. We always had home cooked meals, three a day. She insisted that all homework be completed before any other activity in the afternoon. I kept my grades up, and she let me go into soccer. I was able to buy my cleats and soccer uniform to be on the team. That's something lots of kids like me don't get to do."

"That's good to hear. Anything else?"

Jenn swallowed again and looked at the table. She shook her head and Hadleigh had this weird feeling there was, but she either couldn't or wouldn't say anything.

Hadleigh smiled at Jenn, "It's okay for you to tell us, Jenn. We're not going to tell on you or let anyone know you mentioned anything. We've just had some..." She looked at

Van, not sure she was telling the truth, because she might have to testify in court.

Van stepped in. "Jenn, I work for an organization that stops pedophiles, child traffickers, and child molesters. My job, always, is to protect children. And, I'm very good at it. I tell you this because I want you to know that you are not in trouble in any way for anything. But, knowing that, I'd appreciate it if you would tell us if there's something going on at the Connerts' that we should be aware of. For instance, is someone there taking pictures of children?"

Jenn froze and stared at Van for a long time. Slowly her head shook but she said nothing.

Hadleigh softly added, "We don't want any children to be harmed. Ever. And we've been alerted to some activity in that house that concerns us."

Jenn shook her head, then her eyes dropped to the table-top. Mrs. Janssen leaned over and hugged Jenn to her, rubbing her back and telling her it was okay. After they had embraced for some time Mrs. Janssen looked Jenn in the eyes. "Honey, if there is something, please tell them."

Jenn looked into Mrs. Janssen's eyes and a tear slid down her cheek. But all she did was shake her head no.

Hadleigh's heart hurt. Something had happened in that house with this poor girl. At least they knew something had happened just by the way Jenn behaved, but they still didn't have any evidence.

Van's phone rang; he looked at the readout and ended the call. Just as he was about to put the phone back in his pocket, it started to ring again. He looked once more then stood. "I'm sorry, I have to take this call. Please excuse me."

Mrs. Janssen smiled a shaky smile. "Of course."

"Give me a second."

Hadleigh heard the front door close and looked at Mrs. Janssen. "He does such a good job. His whole team does. They are amazing people."

Jenn looked at her and said, "Is he your boyfriend?"

Hadleigh's cheeks burned as the heat rose up her body. She wondered how to answer that question when Jenn giggled. "It's obvious you know."

Hadleigh smiled, then giggled a bit. "It's new, I guess. So I wasn't sure how to respond."

Mrs. Janssen smiled, "You look good together. I have a good feeling about it. You both work to help kids, that says a lot about the quality people you are. You seem to respect each other, that's important. I've been telling Jenn about that before she goes off to college. Wait for someone who will respect you, who you have things in common with and makes you laugh. I found that with my Frank and we have tried showing Jenn what a good, solid, happy home is like so she sees the value in herself and in waiting for that for herself. I want that for her."

"I want that for her too. Jenn, I really do want only good things for you. I also only want good things for all the kids I find homes for and want to make sure they are good homes. Any information you can share with me is so valuable in working toward that."

Jenn sat up straighter and cleared her throat. "I know." She sniffed. "Thank you."

The front door opened and Van walked back into the room. Hadleigh could tell the news he'd gotten wasn't great. His jaw was tight, his posture was tight, his movements almost seemed wooden. He sat in his chair and glanced at her briefly, then turned to Jenn. "Jenn, did you ever meet Mrs. Connert's brother, Brent Jennings?"

"I heard her talking about him. I overheard her on the phone speaking with him from time to time."

"Do you think they had a good relationship?"

Jenn shrugged. "I guess. She never yelled at him or he her. Usually, she'd just ask where he was and how long he'd be there. Stuff like that."

Van nodded. "Nothing about pictures or anything like that?"

Jenn's cheeks turned bright pink. "No." It came out as a whisper.

"Thank you." Van looked at Hadleigh. "Do you have any other questions, Hadleigh?"

She smiled at him. "No."

He nodded and turned to Mrs. Janssen. "We'll leave you be then. I imagine you're packing and getting things ready to take off for college. Good luck to you Jenn."

He pulled a card from his pocket with his name and phone number and a triangular symbol at the upper left corner in silver with an angular picture of a wolf in it. "If you think of anything that you think can help us or help other young girls and boys who might be placed with the Conners, please give me a call."

"Okay."

Van stood then and pulled Hadleigh's chair away as she stood. He reached across the table and shook Mrs. Janssen's hand, then Jenn's. Hadleigh did the same, "Thank you for your time."

His hand was at the small of her back as they walked through the living room. He opened the door and let her step out ahead of him, then he followed closely until they reached the SUV.

Once inside he said, "I have something for you to look at."

41

He pulled his laptop from its hiding place in the center console, opened the lid and logged on. Typing his password into the RAPTOR software, he pulled up the pictures Piper had just sent him, then turned the laptop around to show Hadleigh.

She gasped when she saw the nude photos of Jenn Owens as a fourteen-year-old girl. There she lay on a red sheet or backdrop, some of them demure, some of them outright bawdy, all of them inappropriate. On some of them she had a wooden wall for a backdrop. Some of them showed just a white background.

"Do you recognize any of those backgrounds?"

Hadleigh's eyes welled with tears as she looked at this little girl with makeup on, hair done, trying hard to look ten years older than she was. Shiny lips and eyeliner around her eyes, Van had been sickened when Piper sent them over to him.

"That red sheet looks like the one I saw in the Connerts' upstairs bedroom."

"Any of the other backgrounds look familiar? How about that wooden wall?"

Hadleigh shook her head then looked away from the laptop. "That's gross."

"Yes. It is."

He closed the lid on his computer, then pushed the Bluetooth button on his steering wheel before starting his car and beginning to drive back to town.

"I told Piper and Caiden where we were going and Piper ran a scan from her photo in the system on the dark web and found these. I'm guessing they're about four years old so that puts her at the Connerts' home."

He turned onto the main road. "I'm also assuming she clammed up tight when we asked if Brent was taking pictures of her; he quite likely threatened her if she ever told."

"That fucking bastard." She swiped at the tears on her cheeks. "He's a wolf in sheep's clothing for sure. That son of a bitch."

"It certainly seems like it, doesn't it?"

"It does."

He drove back to town, more eager now than ever to meet Marco48 and put that son of a bitch away. A red sheet or background wasn't enough to sew up a conviction, though. Maybe Leslie would be more willing to tell them something. They'd have to hope for that now.

His phone rang and he tapped the answer icon. "Keach."

"Hey Van, it's Charly. So, the California police have caught up to Brent Jennings. He doesn't have any kids with him. He also said Miguel had a crush on Autumn and vice versa. He'd come over to the house to talk to her. Sometimes they'd sit on the back porch and chat. That's all he knew."

"Thanks Charly. Did he have any idea where they may be?"

"No. He said he doesn't know a Janine, either. He was only at the house for a few days. Police believe him. He was able to show them texts showing that he was indeed called back to work."

"Okay."

Charly asked, "What's up now?"

He glanced at Hadleigh then back to the road. "Hadleigh managed to set up an appointment with Marco48 tonight. He wants to meet at the Neighborhood Cafe."

Charly gasped on the other end of the line. "Are you friggin kidding me? Right across the street? That's pretty ballsy."

"Yes, it is. What do you make of that?"

Charly was quiet for a while then she said, "He's either going to make one last big splash, or take one more kid to sell and then ditch town."

He took a deep breath. "That's what I was thinking. I'm coming back to headquarters right now. I'm bringing Hadleigh."

"Looking forward to seeing you both."

The call ended and he reached for Hadleigh's hand. He laced their fingers and stroked her palm lightly with his thumb, trying to sooth away the visible tension that carried all the way up to her tightly clenched jaw.

"Hey, what's up?"

"I'm steaming mad. I've been so wrong about this family. It makes me doubt myself and my ability to see what I need to see. I'm also so fucking mad that I might get fired from a shitty job that is supposed to help kids and yet seems more concerned about keeping social workers in a neat and tidy little box than helping kids."

He chuckled, "You need to be mad. You need it to do what needs to be done."

She turned. "What does that mean?"

"We're about to bring down a disgusting pedophile tonight. You need anger so you don't soften when he starts begging and pleading with you that he'll never do it again. They either do that thinking it will save their necks or they clam up. Either way, you need your anger. Hug that bitch for all she's worth right now."

Hadleigh smiled which made him laugh. He turned up the street where RAPTOR was housed, and pushed the button on his visor to open the gates. He drove through them to the garage, and opened the door by touching another button on his visor.

Once parked, he grabbed his laptop from the console, smiling at Hadleigh's expression of disbelief.

He helped her out as usual because he wanted to touch her once again, then took her hand and led her to the door.

"So, I should warn you, my co-workers are going to be interested in you. Brace yourself. They're all great, but still, you'll be stared at and assessed."

"Damn, I likely look like shit."

He stopped and turned her to face him. "You look stunning. They'll love you. And, you already know Charly, so that should help."

"How many co-workers do you have?"

"Eight."

He kissed her lips, then turned and opened the door. They were almost run over by Ted, Anders, Callie, and Diego.

"Whoa, hold up, what's going on?" He laughed.

Ted flew past him, then turned and came back for a scratch behind his ears.

He looked over at Hadleigh. "This is Ted. Diego's dog." He pointed to Diego. "This is Diego, Ted's human." Diego laughed. "Those two munchkins over there are Anders and Callie, Diego's kids."

"Hi Ted, Diego, Anders, and Callie," Hadleigh responded.

"Guys, this is Hadleigh."

Anders and Callie yelled, "Hi," from the back of the garage, where they disappeared into Diego's truck. Diego laughed and reached out his hand. "Nice to meet you,

Hadleigh. The munchkins are hot for ice cream and Shelby is hot for a nap, so, I'm on dad duty for an hour or so."

Hadleigh laughed. "Not a bad way to have duty; you get to fill them with ice cream. That's the fun stuff."

Diego laughed. "That's my evil plan. See you guys in a little while."

Diego whistled and Ted followed him to his truck. He turned to Hadleigh with an indulgent grin. "Those kids are great, you'll like them."

"Do they all live here?"

"Yep. For now, anyway. They're planning to build a house in the next year or so, but they have some stuff to clean up with Shelby's sister's estate. I'll tell you about it later. Let's go meet everyone else."

They entered the house from the garage door and into the kitchen area. The aromas that emerged were mouth-watering. Sheldon turned at the sound of the door and nodded. "Hey Van. Scalloped potatoes and ham tonight, which Callie and Anders wrinkled their noses at."

Van laughed. "Sheldon, this is Hadleigh Watterson. Hadleigh won't wrinkle her nose up at scalloped potatoes and ham."

"No, I won't, it smells delicious."

Sheldon nodded as he continued cutting up cubes of ham. "Thank you. Dinner in an hour."

They made their way through the kitchen toward the hallway leading to the elevators when Sheldon added, "Nice to meet you, Hadleigh."

She smiled at him and he smiled back; his eyes darted to Van's and a little twinkle could be seen in Sheldon's gaze.

Van placed his hand on the small of Hadleigh's back, maybe a bit protective, but he didn't care. They walked to the elevator and he waved his watch in front of the black panel on the wall.

The doors opened and he motioned for Hadleigh to step in first, then he followed. He pushed the button to the conference level and pulled her into his arms. "This feels good."

"It does." She stood on her toes and kissed his lips. Soft wet kisses that made his heart race.

The doors opened, and he walked her to the conference room. He opened the door to a room buzzing with activity.

"Wow," she whispered.

"Yeah."

Walking her to the Cyber team's computer section, he introduced Hadleigh to Piper, Caiden, and Deacon. Then he walked Hadleigh straight back to Emmy.

"Emmy, this is Hadleigh. Hadleigh, Emmy is our commander-in-chief and the reason RAPTOR started. She's smart, capable, rock solid, and a great boss."

Emmy laughed. "What am I going to owe you for that introduction? Nice to meet you, Hadleigh."

Van laughed then steered Hadleigh to the other side of the room where Charly, Falcon, and Creed were working away. He introduced them all to Hadleigh, then asked, "What's happening? There's a ton of activity going on."

Charly started, "Yep, so Piper said she told you about the pictures of Jenn Owens. And you know about Brent Jennings, so the newest information is that we tracked the phone Autumn Lynn has and she's been located at the Dip N' Twist. You found that back room where Jennings was taking pictures of Janine. I'm guessing she's hiding out there. Who's up for ice cream?"

"Shit, Diego is on his way to get Callie and Anders ice cream."

"I'll call him and tell him not to go there, we'll be swinging in to take the kids."

"What about Miguel?"

"We got a phone number for him too from his school computer. His tracking shows him at the Dip N' Twist as well."

He looked at Hadleigh, "Show time. Are you ready?"

"Yes, I'm ready. Let's go get them."

"This might be it for you Hadleigh, you could get fired for stepping this far outside of the box they've put you in."

Hadleigh looked at Charly and Falcon, who turned to watch her reaction. She smiled and said, "Totally worth it to save those kids."

42

H adleigh was both excited and nervous. She'd never in her life done anything like this. Never. Never dreamed she would. She didn't figure herself to be a badass. But she was eager to watch Van and his team members do their job. She was eager to get the kids to safety. She was eager to tell Lucy—to tell the state —to shove their shitty job up their asses. She'd find something else. Suddenly, working under the types of rules they had held little appeal. She'd find a job where she could help kids and actually make a difference.

They walked out of the building and into their separate vehicles. She got into the passenger side of Van's SUV and watched as Charly and Falcon jumped into his truck. Emmy had said to call her if they needed her assistance, but she was on the trail of someone else she was tailing and told them to be ready once they finished up this job; there were more jobs coming in. Something about getting the agency's contract and new jobs. Van said he'd fill her in. They had a lot of filling in to do in the coming days and she was looking forward to it.

He turned the vehicle out of the driveway and onto the main road that would take them into town. They drove a few miles and he started talking.

"When we get there, we'll park a block down. Charly and Falcon will park in the back. They're calling Rory right now to have him on standby, which really means he'll be there about ten minutes after we get there. He'll take the kids to a foster home to be taken care of until we know what will happen in the long term. Miguel is not a foster; his parents will be called as soon as we have him and they'll have to go to the police station to pick him up."

"Okay."

"When we get there Hadleigh, you need to stay back and let us do our work. Sometimes these things are easy, sometimes the kids run, kick, scream, yell, or the people helping them get in the way thinking they are helping. I can't do my job if I'm worried you're in danger. Promise me."

"I promise."

"As soon as we have the kids wrapped up, we'll head over to the coffee shop and set up our positions much like we're doing here at the ice cream shop with Charly and Falcon. We'll then arrest Marco48 and take that bastard in. Rory and his team will go in and sweep the Connerts' home, gather evidence and do what the police do."

"How do you get paid for this work?"

He smiled. "That agency that Emmy mentioned, they are the agency that paid us when we all worked for the government. They are secretive about how they are funded, and we don't care. We stole that contract from the government because they had a bunch of assholes taking money under the table for these kids. That's why we all quit. Now, we'll be paid and paid handsomely to do what we do. Things are definitely looking up for RAPTOR and that's all good. That means we'll be able to afford some of the fun toys GHOST has in terms of cool equipment. Plus, we'll all get raises. Bonus right there."

"Wow. That's really cool. I assume you'll also fill me in on what GHOST is?" He nodded then she watched his smile fade as they neared the ice cream shop and she knew somehow that he was getting into his work mode.

She didn't want to get in his way, but she was eager to see what they did. She also wanted Autumn safe and sound and she hoped they'd be able to find a place where she would be. It sickened her to think that she'd placed Autumn, and countless other kids, in the Connerts' home believing they were a good family only to find a pervert lived in the home. For ten years she'd been fooled and she felt stupid and inept because of it.

Van pulled to the curb a block away and grabbed a pistol from inside his console. He loaded it, holstered it in his ankle holster, then pulled out another pistol. He repeated his motions from previously and then holstered that gun on his hip. He looked over at her, leaned in and kissed her. "Ready?"

"Yes."

They exited the vehicle. She didn't wait for him to open her door, they were working now, all dating behaviors were off the table, and she was fine with that. They walked in silence to the ice cream shop. He took her hand in his and they acted the couple out for an ice cream. Normally they would be.

Once they reached the door, he looked down at her. "We'll get a table at the back, you stay there. Charly and Falcon will go in the back door. I found it earlier this week. The kids may run out, the employees may make a ruckus, just stay put."

"I will, Van. I promise."

He opened the door and she walked in. He walked them to a table against the far wall, but not all the way to the back. She sat at the table, with her back to the front of the store, and he pulled his phone from his back pocket and texted Charly. "Ready."

He turned his phone to show her, a thumbs up was his reply. She watched the kitchen door and the front door and the patrons in the store. There were eight of them.

Soon screaming could be heard from the back, and a couple of the patrons stood up and looked toward the front of the store. More screams, slamming doors and yelling could be heard and soon the girl that had been behind the counter when they'd been there yesterday came running out of the kitchen door. Van jumped up and ran to catch her, she kicked and screamed and kicked some more. She saw him visibly grimace as a couple of her back kicks hit his shin. He wrapped his arms around her, locking her arms to her sides and she reared her head

back and tried to hit him in the nose. He must have antici-
pated it as his head flew back before she could connect
and she must have hurt her neck because she howled and
stopped fighting.

He lay her on the floor, and pulled her hands behind her
back and a police officer entered the front door at that
time and took over.

Van stood and waited to make sure the officer had her
under control, then he looked over to see she'd remained
where he told her. He nodded and disappeared through
the door to the kitchen area and Hadleigh's stomach
knotted.

43

V an took a deep breath as he walked through the door to the back area. He saw Charly struggling with a young boy, who he assumed was Miguel. She was small but mighty and Miguel was still shorter than Charly and luckily, his muscles not fully developed, though he did put up a fight. It seemed she was handling him the best she could so he continued to the room he'd found where Jennings was taking pictures. There he found Falcon Montgomery kneeling on the floor next to Autumn Lynn, who lay on her belly crying.

"You got this Falcon?"

"Yeah, we're good." He rose and walked out to the hallway where a loud crash had just sounded. Seeing Charly pushing Miguel against the wall, face first, one arm twisted behind his back, and a metal bucket still rolling on the ground at her feet, he hesitated to take over. Charly didn't like being treated as if she were weak.

Charly turned her head and looked at him. "This kid has some fight."

"Need help?"

"Wouldn't hurt." She grunted.

Van walked to them, pressed his forearm across Miguel's shoulder blades holding him tightly to the wall, then nodded to Charly, who stepped back, still holding Miguel's hands behind his shoulders for Van to take. Once he had a good grip on them, Charly stepped back.

"Did you get the girl whose parents own this place?"

"Yeah. A cop has her out front."

"Detective Bowers?"

Van snickered. "Sorry, no."

Miguel fought a little harder and Van pushed on him a bit more.

"Charly, go out and see if there are more cops coming in to take these kids to the station."

Miguel finally spoke. "I don't want to go to the station."

"Sorry bud, but you're a runaway and you'll have to go in until your parents come to get you."

"That's messed up man."

"What's messed up is you running away and making your parents sick with worry."

The back door opened and three police officers entered.

One of them was Detective Bowers. Charly would be thrilled to see him. He grinned as Bowers approached. "Need some help with this scrappy little dude?"

Van grinned. "That would be nice. Though Charly largely had him all wrapped up before I got here."

Sam Bowers was an impressive man, even by other men's standards. His smile was broad when Van had mentioned Charly's name and Van made a mental note that maybe they should get it out of their system. But that was none of his business.

Sam stepped forward and clipped a cuff on one of Miguel's wrists, then quickly clipped the second cuff on with ease. Van stepped away and Miguel turned as if he'd bolt only to see Sam Bowers and his sheer size in his way. The man was massive. Miguel then turned his face to the wall and leaned his forehead against the aging wood.

The front door to the hallway opened and Charly walked back into the area.

"All good out..."

She looked up and saw Sam Bowers standing next to Van and Miguel and froze.

Van chuckled and stepped back. "I'll go check on Hadleigh."

On his way to the door, he stopped at the door to the kitchen and looked inside. There were two younger kids standing at the doorway, their eyes large and round, staring.

"You have anything on the stove right now?"

Both kids shook their heads.

"Come on out here and take a seat. You'll need to make a statement to police."

They looked at each other and hesitated.

"Let's go. You aren't in trouble, but clearly, no one is ordering anything right now, so you may as well come out and sit."

They each walked to the doorway, silent as monks, and Van followed them out. Two officers sat them each at different tables across the room to ask them questions.

Van looked to the table where Hadleigh had been and smiled when he found her sitting right where he'd left her.

"Thank you for staying put," he said as he sat at the table with her.

"Of course."

He looked into her eyes and smiled. "We have Miguel and Autumn in the back. Police have them now and they will be taken first to the station, then Miguel will go home with his parents and Autumn will go to another foster home temporarily until a suitable one can be found for her."

"I'm glad they were found and not kidnapped."

"Me too. But Janine isn't back there. So she's still out and about somewhere."

Hadleigh nodded. "I hope she just ran away and isn't in the hands of some creep."

"Me too."

"Do we leave now?"

Van looked at the kids speaking with police. Falcon Montgomery walked into the restaurant from the back hallway, Van caught his attention and walked to where they were seated.

He pulled a chair up to the table, "Both Miguel and Autumn are on their way to the station. Charly's making eyes at Bowers. And, he's making eyes back at her, so, there's that."

"Who's Bowers?" Hadleigh asked.

Falcon looked at Hadleigh, his brows in the air. "You haven't seen Sam Bowers?"

"No."

Falcon then looked at Van. "You scared she'll be chasing after Bowers or something?"

Van laughed. "No. At least I don't think so. We just haven't had the opportunity."

As if on cue, Sam Bowers walked from the back hallway, Charly beside him with a grin on her face.

"Looks like opportunity just walked in."

Hadleigh turned her head to follow Falcon's line of sight. She locked on Sam Bowers and Van watched in amusement as she stared. Her mouth dropped open.

Seeing Charly standing next to Bowers was funny. He was easily six foot-nine and she was five-two. Both were blonde, but Charly was petite, Bowers was massive. They didn't fit, and then again, they did.

Bowers and Charly walked up to their table.

"You can take off if you like, we have this under control. I understand we have another bust coming up in an hour or so." Bowers boomed.

Van responded, still grinning at the look on Hadleigh's face. "Yes, we'll be at the Neighborhood Cafe and I assume we'll see you there."

Bowers nodded. "Richards will be there as well, he was stuck in a situation when we came here."

Van's gaze landed on Charly, who was unusually quiet. He then switched his gaze to Falcon who chuckled. Falcon stood and shook hands with Bowers, "See you later."

Van stood and Hadleigh slowly followed suit. "Bowers, I'd like you to meet Hadleigh Watterson. Hadleigh, Sam Bowers."

"Nice meeting you," she mumbled.

Van nodded at Bowers, held his hand out for Hadleigh, and the instant she took his hand he pulled her along to the door. He didn't need her pining away for Bowers, too.

44

The closer they got to the Neighborhood Cafe, the more Hadleigh's tummy twisted and turned. There was a point where she almost asked Van to stop so she could throw up. She practiced deep breathing exercises to calm her stomach and it seemed to help. She was coming face to face with a man she'd thought was such a good man all these years and she now knew was anything but. Her newfound disgust of this man was taking over her nervous system.

Van turned to look at her. "You okay?"

"Yeah. Just nervous."

He nodded. "So, we'll do the same thing we did this last time. You stay at the table while this all goes down. You know you're HanMarn but he doesn't. And, if he sees you anywhere close, he may be spooked and run away. We don't want that."

"Right. Okay."

She let out a long breath and looked out the window. Van pulled onto Station Street and she watched the street with interest. It looked the same as it always did, though she didn't know what she expected, except that it seemed darker, dirtier, awful. That of course, was her imagination in knowing what was going on across the street from the Neighborhood Cafe.

Van parked his car two blocks down the street. "We'll walk in from here."

"Do you think he'll be watching?"

"I wouldn't think so, his actions are such that he is invincible, but you bring up a good point."

He restarted his SUV and drove down the street, turned right at the end and right again to go around the block. "We'll go in from the back way."

She reminded herself to breathe regularly again, realizing she'd been holding her breath. Van parked his SUV on the side of the street, and turned off the ignition. He turned to her and looked directly into her eyes.

"You can stay in here if you want."

She shook her head, "No, I want to see him as he's handcuffed and taken away."

He reached over and cupped her jaw in his hand and stared into her eyes.

"I love you, Hadleigh. I think I fell in love with you when I first met you. But I know I love you now."

She looked deep into his eyes, even though one cloudy, it tried to see her. His right eye was clear and blue and held his feelings in there. She could see it. He was serious.

"I love you, too, Van. It's almost like it just was! We were supposed to be together; everything has been so natural and strong and I feel like even though things are so new with us, they aren't. Do you know what I mean?"

He leaned forward and kissed her. "I do. I know exactly what you mean."

He kissed her again and she tried without words to show him that she meant it. She loved him.

When he pulled away, he let out a breath. "Okay, let's do this so we can drive to Valparaiso and hit a hotel room. I want to hold you all night long."

"That sounds fantastic."

He chuckled and opened his door. She opened hers and got out, then met him at the curb where they walked hand in hand toward the coffee shop. The darkness of moments before faded away as she felt like she glowed from Van's admission that he loved her. She'd finally, after all these years, found the man of her dreams.

They walked around to the front of the coffee shop and she forced herself not to look at the Connerts' house. After they'd entered, he found them a seat at a table that was close to the front door.

They sat at the table, Van facing most of the shop, Hadleigh facing the front door. Van pulled his phone out and texted Charly. "Ready."

He waited until he got the thumbs up from Charly, showed her the phone and smiled.

"Stay here, Hadleigh."

She nodded and swallowed a giant lump that had formed in her throat.

The door opened and she about jumped out of her skin when the bell rang. Charly walked in, a big smile on her face and a skip in her step. She walked to their table and sat across from Hadleigh, blocking her view of the front door.

Soon, Falcon walked into the coffee shop and sat in the fourth chair. A waitress came over and took their order then walked away.

Charly started the conversation; softly she said, "So, there isn't a back door like at the ice cream shop. The one that's back there can only be opened from the inside, no handle on the outside. I don't know what Marco48 has in mind, or if his intent is just to watch how busy it is here, but I think we should drink a cup of coffee and chat like friends. If he doesn't come, we give him until about thirty minutes after, then Falcon and I will go snoop around the house and see what's up. Unless Cyber team sees something on the cameras watching the house first."

Van nodded. "Did Cyber confirm that the IP we had for Marco48 is still coming from the Connerts?"

"Yes, they've confirmed each time he comments online."

Falcon leaned in. "Cyber is so good, they've even looked at the times he's commenting to see if it's during the day and from his phone or his home computer. Those guys are good."

Their order was delivered and Hadleigh tried relaxing and acting casual; each of the people at the table with her seemed to manage it.

Van asked Charly, "So you and Bowers going out?"

"No." Charly said rather snappily.

"You look at him like you're going out."

Charly sat back in her chair and shrugged. "I don't think he's interested. Might be this." She lifted her left arm up, her prosthetic arm.

Falcon looked at Charly then her arm, then back at Charly. "Nah, it isn't that. It's that you look at him like you've already planned the wedding."

Charly smacked Falcon on the arm. "I do not."

Van and Falcon both laughed and Charly pouted. Though, as pouts go, Hadleigh wished she could look as cute as Charly when she pouted.

Charly looked at Hadleigh, "What do you think?"

Hadleigh raised her hands up in the air. "Nope. I don't want to get involved in this."

"Tell me, do I look at Bowers all sappy like?"

Hadleigh raised her right shoulder then let it fall.

"Oh my God, you think I do."

The door opened and Hadleigh stiffened.

45

Customers came and went, but Marco48, or Melvyn Connert, didn't. After more than fifty minutes Falcon grabbed his empty cup and stood.

"I'm going over and snooping."

Charly followed him. "Me, too."

They exited the coffee shop and Van pulled his phone out of his pocket and lay it on the table in front of him.

"We'll wait till we hear from them, then we'll leave. Something spooked him."

"Do you think he saw us come in?"

"I don't know. There's a lot of traffic in here and it would be impossible to watch every single person."

Van's phone lit up and he looked down to see a text from Piper.

"Marco48 just messaged you online. IP at the house."

Van opened up the app he'd been communicating with Marco48 on and there was the message.

"Meet me tonight?"

"Y. Where?"

He looked at Hadleigh. "Marco48 wants to meet me tonight. Why don't you message him and ask him where he's at?"

Hadleigh pulled up her phone and texted Marco48. After she sent it, she laid her phone on the table and waited.

Her phone lit up with a message, "Sry. Late. Change of plans. Meet me at the empty car garage on Fisk Street in thirty mins."

Hadleigh showed him the message. Van nodded, "Tell him yes."

Van's phone then lit up. "Empty car garage on Fisk in thirty mins."

Van replied, "K."

Hadleigh waited a minute then replied. "K."

Van texted Charly and Falcon and let them know what was going on. Charly responded, "Stay there."

"We're to stay here."

He noticed Hadleigh's hands shaking so he reached over and wrapped his hands around hers on the table. He smiled at her. "You're doing great. It takes a while to get used to this stuff."

"I've been admiring how you all look so casual and I feel like a wreck."

He chuckled. "You're a beautiful wreck then."

He leaned in and kissed her and enjoyed the smile she bestowed on him.

The door opened and Charly and Falcon walked into the coffee shop. After sitting Charly quietly said, "Melvyn just took off in the Cadillac."

Van nodded and pushed his chair back, "Okay. He's on his way to the garage. Do you know which one he's talking about?"

Falcon said, "Yeah, there used to be a car repair garage on Fisk Street years ago. It's been empty for years now. I don't know how he's getting in there or if he is, he might just be trying to figure out if someone's on to him. He'd likely expect a kid to either ride a bicycle or walk up to the garage."

Charly spoke up. "That's me. I've got a beanie in the truck, and a sweat shirt. Drop me off a couple blocks away around the corner and I'll walk up to the garage."

Van looked at Falcon, who nodded. "Okay, let's go."

Falcon responded, "We'll alert Rory."

They all stood and he and Hadleigh left first. He took her hand once again, and they walked around the corner to the back of the lot. After they'd cleared the building, he wrapped his arm around her shoulder and pulled her into his body. He always felt better when he was holding Hadleigh close.

She wrapped her arm around his waist and lay her head against his chest as they walked. He could have walked for hours like this.

He opened the passenger door for her and watched as she gracefully slid inside. Walking around the front of the SUV he smiled; life was pretty great right now.

They drove down the street slowly, then crossed the first intersection. By the second intersection, something didn't feel right to him. A prickling at the base of his neck started to nag at him and his unease grew the closer they got to Fisk Street.

He jabbed at the Bluetooth icon on his steering wheel and waited for the robotic voice to ask what he wanted.

"Call HQ."

The phone rang once, "Smythe."

"Hey Deac, can you do a check for me?"

"Sure."

"There's a garage on Fisk Street, it used to be a business. Now it's empty. Can you see if the Connerts or JenMark owns it or anything on Fisk Street?"

"You bet. I'll call you right back."

He turned onto Fisk Street and parked at the edge of the street. They were around four blocks away from the garage.

Hadleigh turned to look at him and he rubbed the back of his neck.

"What's wrong?"

"It doesn't feel right. Since I lost my sight, I get this prickling on the back of my neck when things aren't right. God's way of helping me out I guess. I've got that now."

Hadleigh looked up the street and saw Charly walking from the other direction. She pointed and Van let out a long breath.

"This isn't good."

He opened his door and jumped out of the SUV. "Stay here Hadleigh. Don't leave this vehicle."

"But..."

"Don't. Leave."

He walked up the street on the opposite side of the garage and watched Charly make her way toward the garage. His phone buzzed in his pocket and he pulled it out halfway to read the screen. "Garage owned by JenMark LLC. Purchased ten years ago."

He'd been taking pictures in the garage. Van checked the neighborhood around the garage. No houses anymore. The street where he'd parked was populated, but just a block up, it looked deserted. It looked like an abandoned section of town with no witnesses, no one to see what was going on.

He picked up his pace just as Charly got to the door and knocked. She waited, then stepped off the concrete and walked to the decrepit garage doors. She rose up on her toes to look in the small rectangle windows in the door. She couldn't reach the windows.

Van looked around for the white Cadillac. It wasn't on this street. He pulled his phone from his pocket and called Falcon.

"Yeah."

"I can't see the Caddy. You?"

There was a slight pause then, "No."

"Something's wrong."

That's when he heard gunshots but they didn't come from the garage. They came from...He turned his head toward his SUV and saw the shooter standing just behind his SUV, a gun pointed at...

Hadleigh.

46

H adleigh's heart raced as if she'd just run a marathon. She watched Van cross the street then walk toward the garage. She saw Charly walk up to the door. Her eyes darted back and forth between Van and Charly.

Something in the mirror caught her eye and she ducked. That's when tiny shards of glass sprayed over her as she lay on the seat. Someone had shot at her.

Her ears rang from the shot so close to her. Her breathing came in spurts, her nostrils filled with gunshot residue and she didn't know if the shooter was still alongside the car and going to shoot her point blank or not. If she lifted her head right now would he shoot her? She slid down until she was curled up on the floor on the passenger side.

Then there were more shots, many more. Another one hit the SUV, she could hear the sound of it as it hit, but she didn't think she'd been hit. She raised her hands over her head and tried to remain as small as she could. Then, silence.

It seemed like an eternity and she was frozen in a state of confusion. Was the shooter waiting for her to lift her head? She didn't have her own weapon. She had no way to fight back against a gun except to hope that Van would get back and help her before she was killed.

Her door was suddenly opened and she screamed. Hands reached in for her and she slapped them back. "No. Leave me alone. No."

"Hey, it's me. Van. Hadleigh, I'm here to help you."

His hands rubbed over her back as she tried to unroll herself from the floor of the SUV. Her hands shook, her eyes were blurry, tears slid down her cheeks as if a faucet were running. Van's strong hands reached in and pulled her from the floor. She managed to put an arm on the seat and lift herself up enough that he reached in and pulled her out.

He walked to the grass in a nearby yard; she turned in his arms and wrapped her arms around his neck. He gently set her legs on the ground but she couldn't let go of him. She started hyperventilating instantly upon her feet touching the ground and Van wrapped his arms solidly around her and pulled her tightly into his body.

She could hear the voices of others around them but she couldn't understand their words. She didn't care right then—she just wanted Van to hold her and feel him against her.

Sirens in the distance brought her around to the here and now and she loosened her grip on Van's neck.

"Who shot at me?"

Van held her head in his hands, forcing her to look at him. "Hey, first you. Have you been hit?"

"No. I don't think so."

He swiped gently at her face. "You have small cuts on your face and arms from the glass. Just think for a moment and make sure you weren't hit somewhere."

He stepped back and looked at her body for signs of a gunshot wound, but found none.

"Who shot at me?"

Van took a deep breath and let it out. "Bethany."

"Bethany?" She shook her head. "Bethany? As is Bethany Connert?"

"Yeah."

"Where's Melvyn?"

"Police are looking for him."

Hadleigh leaned around Van to see the ambulance lifting a gurney with a body on it, a sheet pulled over its head. "I want to see her."

"Why?"

"I need to know she isn't going to hurt me ever again."

"She won't Hadleigh. She's dead."

Hadleigh blinked a few times.

"Dead?"

She pulled away and walked to the gurney; Van took her hand and went with her.

As they approached the gurney, one of the EMTs spoke. "Ma'am do you need medical assistance?"

Hadleigh shook her head. "No."

Van addressed the EMT in charge. "She wants to see the victim."

The EMT, a young man in his early twenties, looked at her then again at Van. "You sure?"

"Yes."

He pulled back the sheet and Hadleigh looked at Bethany's face. Her eyes were open but there was no life. She had blood splattered on her face but nothing else to show the violence that had just happened here.

Hadleigh stepped back and took a deep breath. For the first time she looked at Van's SUV, the back window shot out, and the passenger back window shot out too. Charly stood to the side speaking with a police officer as did Falcon. Van looked at her, "Hadleigh, are you okay?"

"Yes. I'm fine."

"We'll have to go to the police department and tell them what happened. Are you able to get into the back of the squad car?"

She nodded. She felt sort of numb. "Can I get my purse from your car?"

"An officer will retrieve it." He walked them over to the officer waiting for them. "Hadleigh is asking if she can get her purse from the vehicle."

"Where is it ma'am?"

"It's on the passenger floor."

"Do you have a weapon in it?"

She shook her head. He reached in and pulled her purse from under the seat. Her eyes followed his movements and she wondered how she'd fit in that small spot.

Van's arm snaked around her shoulder, interrupting her musings as he gently steered her to the waiting squad car.

He helped her in the back of the squad, then walked around and got into the other side.

The officer who had been waiting got into the squad. She sat stone-still, processing what had just happened and still fuzzy on many details.

"Was it Bethany who was taking the pictures?"

"We still don't know. But police officers are on their way to speak with Jenn Owens, Amber Lynn, and Leslie Knot. Now that the threat is gone, or so it would seem, they may be more willing to say something so we can wrap this up.

The police radio in the squad chirped and dispatch said, "Melvyn Connert is in custody."

Hadleigh relaxed into the back of the seat. Then she said to the officer, "There is a baby in the Connerts' home, his name is Henry and he's ten months old. Do they have him?"

The officer asked dispatch if Melvyn had a baby with him. The reply came back, "No."

The officer then replied, "Dispatch, please send a squad to the Connerts' home for a welfare check. There is a baby there, he may be with a sitter. Or, he may be on his own."

"Roger."

47

D onovan woke up with Hadleigh sleeping peacefully in his arms. They'd come back to RAPTOR last night to debrief Emmy and the team and they'd both been so tired they went up to his apartment and stayed the night. She'd tossed and turned most of the night, but finally fell into a deep sleep around two thirty in the morning. He held her close to him which seemed to help settle her.

A quick look at his watch told him it was now six thirty in the morning.

Hadleigh rolled over and faced him, her face still puffy from lack of sleep, but as beautiful as ever. "I like sleeping with you."

He smiled, "I like sleeping with you."

"What do we have to do today?"

"I'd like to get dressed and go see what information has been gathered overnight. Hopefully we'll have a fuller picture of what was going on in that house all this time. From there, you should call Lucy and see what's going to happen with your job."

Hadleigh sat up and stretched. "I already know what's going to happen with my job. They can shove it. I don't know if I have the fortitude to do what you do, but I'm a social worker. It seems to me there is something I can do here. When you bring kids in, there must be something I can do for them. I can do research; I can do something. I like the fact that you all get to color outside of the lines. I want to color outside the lines myself."

He smiled at her. "You don't think you have fortitude?"

"Well, I didn't like being shot at."

"No one does, Hadleigh."

"But my first reaction was to cower down and cover my head, yours was to shoot back and protect."

"That's my training. It's also that I love you and I don't want to live without you, so I was willing to do anything to save you."

Hadleigh turned to look at him. She'd slept in one of his t-shirts and her nipples poked at the fabric enticingly this morning. His eyes dropped down to look and she laughed.

"Even though you can't have a conversation with me without looking at my boobs, I don't want to live without you either."

"You have them poking out at me just begging to be looked at."

She lunged for him and he grabbed her, his arms wrapped tightly around her body as he pulled her down on top of him. He kissed her lips, softly at first, but as their kisses became more urgent their bodies grew heated, and since he was already naked it didn't take long to pull that t-shirt from her sexy body, flip her on her back and slide himself inside of her.

He groaned as her warmth encased his cock. She mewled as he filled her, then pulled out and filled her again. They started their dance, their mating, their lovemaking slow and steady as they both enjoyed the feel of the other. As he slid in and out of her, he watched her face, her breasts as they swayed with his movements, then her face again as she grew closer to her orgasm. She looked stunning when she came. He'd take a picture of it one day, that face she made as he made every nerve ending in her body erupt in the carnal pleasures, they both enjoyed.

His skin heated as they moved more rapidly; she was getting close. He pushed in a bit harder and enjoyed her responding sigh as she felt it. He moved faster, his own orgasm coming close, his own release on the verge of spilling into her. Hadleigh moaned as she grabbed at his back, her legs wrapped around his ass, her hips reaching for that feeling. Then she cried out his name as she came and he pumped into her three more times before letting his own orgasm erupt. His body jerked and he kissed the side of her head, her cheek, and her ear.

He kissed her lips briefly, then pulled her with him as he rolled to his side. She sighed and nuzzled his neck as they both rested from their exertion. What a way to wake up in the morning.

After they'd showered, he and Hadleigh emerged from his apartment and headed downstairs, using the staircase instead of the elevator because he wanted to show Hadleigh the entire building. Their staircase wasn't as grand as the GHOST staircase next door, but it was nice and more modern with its wrought iron railings and dark wood. The entryway below was much smaller than the entry next door but it was neat and tidy. The tile floors were clean and the small round table that stood in the center always had a floral arrangement which fit to the season compliments of, Shioban, their housekeeper.

At the bottom of the stairs, the rich aroma of freshly brewed coffee and something delicious baking in the over called them to the kitchen. "Good morning, Sheldon," Van greeted.

"Morning, Van. Morning, Hadleigh. Coffee is brewed and ready over there." He pointed to a counter above a bank of cabinets across from the center island he worked at. "I have freshly baked coffee cake coming out in three minutes." He pointed to the oven behind him. "And scrambled eggs in the warmer in the dining room."

Hadleigh smiled. "Thank you, Sheldon."

He smiled at her and nodded. They prepared coffees and walked into the dining room where Charly and Deacon sat eating their scrambled eggs.

"Morning," Hadleigh greeted.

Charly answered first. "Good morning. Deacon just told me they gathered a ton of information last night."

Deacon smiled. "Morning. We did. After breakfast we can go down. Emmy is already down there."

"Fantastic," he replied. They filled their plates with scrambled eggs, bacon, and toast wedges from the warmers on the buffet, then sat to eat.

The dining room was a place where business was not spoken about, but good conversation was always present and the atmosphere was usually casual.

Anders came walking into the room; Shelby close behind him.

"Good morning," Shelby greeted.

Van replied, "Good morning. Shelby this is Hadleigh Watterson. Hadleigh, Shelby is Diego's wife, and Anders's mother."

Hadleigh smiled, "It's very nice to meet you. Hi Anders; we didn't see each other long yesterday. Did you enjoy your ice cream?"

"Yeah. I got Blue Moon. Callie got chocolate."

Shelby laughed. "But he wore most of it home."

Van's phone alerted him to a text and he looked down to see Emmy's name.

"I have information for you when you're ready."

He responded quickly, "We're finishing up breakfast and will be down."

48

They sat at the conference room table and Emmy sat across from them.

"So, here's what we've been able to gather so far. "Other members of the team began walking over and taking seats at the table as Emmy laid out documents on the table.

"Melvyn Connert was arrested last night after he was picked up. He's not a strong person when it comes to mental fortitude. He quite literally sang like a bird. Bethany had been taking pictures of these kids," she pointed to a list of names on the table, "for many years. We don't need to see the pictures, they're sickening. Apparently, she coaxed them into posing for the pictures by telling the kids that she would sell them. She kept seventy-five percent and gave the kids twenty-five. As you can imagine, foster kids with no one else to guide them and no opportunity to make money jumped at the chance. She threatened them that if they told she'd send the pictures to all of their friends and their birth parents who would never want anything to do with them again. The kids believed her. Over the years she also got the kids she fostered to bring friends home from school and she took their pictures, too. The list, as you can see, is long."

"She made a lot of money on the sale of these pictures. Jenn Owens did talk to police last night and said she'd been with the Connerts for four months and made in that time ten thousand dollars. That's a lot of money. At the time Jenn was fourteen and she didn't like how she felt after she took the pictures. She said she felt dirty. Then she met her, now, foster mother and jumped at the chance to get out of the Connert house. She never said anything because she didn't want anyone to know. When you went to speak with her yesterday, she was petrified someone would find out. When police got there, and told her Bethany had been killed, she shared her story."

Emmy paused and waited to see if anyone had any questions. When no one spoke, she continued. "Melvyn only found out this week. He'd been questioning Bethany about Hadleigh's suspicions and Brent. Apparently, he and Bethany had a regular row yesterday when she told him. Police confiscated Bethany's computer and found all the pictures. Thousands and thousands of them. We also have the names and addresses, or at least emails and IP addresses, that can be traced to the sickos who bought the pictures from her. He got mad and left the house last night, intending to leave for good. He was afraid he'd be arrested as an accomplice. Personally, I don't know how he could live in that house and not know any of this was going on, but he's a little man sitting in his pathetic little world and not paying attention to anything. Apparently. We're still trying to figure it all out."

Hadleigh rubbed her upper arms with her hands in an effort to warm herself.

Van asked, "Is Bethany, Marco48?"

"Yes." Emmy pulled another document from a folder. "Apparently Bethany's father, Mark, was called Marco when he was younger. We don't know where the 48 came from."

"Brent Jennings is cooperating with police in California. He said he knew nothing about what was going on. He's stunned his sister would do anything like this."

Hadleigh asked, "What about Henry? Had he been left home alone last night?"

Emmy's lips thinned as she looked across the table at Hadleigh. "I'm afraid so. He was sleeping in his crib. Bethany likely thought she'd be home before he ever woke up, but she had no one else there to watch him."

Hadleigh sat back hard in the chair and nodded slowly.

Van looked at her and she nodded that she was fine.

He then looked at Emmy. "What about Janine, the other girl who is missing?"

Emmy shook her head. "Bethany did not have pictures of Janine, but Brent remembered her. He was taking pictures of her, though nothing bad; he was trying to decide if that back room could work for a scene in a movie coming up that he is scouting for. He used her because she was the right size and he wanted to see if her size cast the correct shadows and if the room would work. She's a runaway and wanted the money. Alison from the ice cream store, helps the kids out with food and shelter when she can. She has a soft spot for them. She doesn't know where Janine goes when she isn't there, she just allows them to come to the ice cream store when they need her."

Hadleigh looked at Emmy, "Why did Autumn and Miguel run away?"

"Autumn told Miguel about the pictures and he didn't like it. He's very protective of her. He likes her. For a boy of ten, he's shown amazing protective skills. Maybe he'll work for us one day. They ran away and Autumn had some money from Bethany. But, when it came right down to it, two young kids traveling without adults would raise eyebrows. Miguel then decided he should go home and wanted Autumn to come with him. But she was afraid his parents would turn her back in to social services and she didn't want to go. When you found them, they were arguing about what to do. That's why she just gave up."

"What will happen to her?"

"Sadly, she'll go back into the system, but she will be offered counseling and I hope she takes it."

Falcon shook his head. "I always think I've seen it all, and then, shit like this comes up and I feel like I haven't seen anything."

Charly nodded, "Isn't that the friggin' truth?"

Emmy nodded, "I wish we never had to do this type of work but I'm glad we're on it. Also, while you're all here, we did get the agency contract from H.O.W. They are paying us on this one as well and from this point forward, they'll pay us handsomely. Any agency job we do will afford us stellar equipment, and raises for everyone."

Cheers and clapping erupted around the table and Emersyn smiled. "To begin with, I'm hiring a pilot who comes with her own plane. Once we can afford our own, which should be later this year, we'll have our own plane and pilot. That should make us more mobile."

Once again cheers and clapping erupted and Emersyn stood up and took a half bow. As people disbursed Hadleigh asked Emersyn, "May I have a chat with you?"

Emmy turned to her and smiled, "Of course."

Hadleigh looked at Van, "Are you okay with this?"

"I couldn't be happier."

She smiled into his handsome face and nodded. Emmy came and sat at the table and Hadleigh started telling her about her job and that she wanted to work for RAPTOR.

Emmy listened and smiled, "Can I give it some thought? I want to see in what capacity we could use you and make sure we're both happy with the choice."

"Of course. Take the time you need. I still need to go quit my job and then get my stuff out of my office."

Emmy stood once again. "I'll speak with you tomorrow."

CHAPTER 49

Hadleigh walked down the staircase, her hand over her stomach, as she approached the office on the first floor where Emersyn waited for her. She let out a long breath before she reached the door then knocked.

"Come in, Hadleigh."

Hadleigh opened the door and saw a smiling Emersyn stand up from her desk and walk toward her, Emersyn's limp wasn't as pronounced today as it had been yesterday. She held out her hand and Hadleigh gripped it tightly and shook.

"We didn't actually formally meet, so I thought I'd rectify that. Let's sit, shall we?"

Emmy walked toward the brown leather sofa in her office across from her desk. It had been in her apartment when she was in the service, a splurge purchase after a tough mission. She wanted it down here, instead of in her apartment here at the compound, because she loved looking at it and it reminded her of what she'd accomplished.

"I'm not sure what Van has shared with you about what we do. I know you've seen firsthand how dangerous it can get. And I know you have the heart for the kids we save. But, sometimes, we can't save them. It's heartbreaking and we're trying to keep that to the lowest number possible, but sometimes, we...can't."

Emmy swallowed and Hadleigh loved her a bit more for her compassion and heart.

"He told me a bit about what you do. He's been filling me in on GHOST and your connection to them through your Uncle Gaige. I know everyone on staff is in some way handicapped or differently abled and I admire that. I honestly haven't seen anything any of you can't do as a team, so I'm thrilled that you've made it a point to hire only wounded veterans. And," she shrugged, "I know I'm not one."

Emmy smiled. "I would never not hire a quality person because they weren't disabled in some way, Hadleigh. First and foremost, I want the best of the best. I happen to think that the team I have here is the best at what they do because of what we've each been through. We're all, in some ways, differently abled, including you. It's just that most of us have our differences on the outside."

Hadleigh nodded. "That makes sense."

"So, I went over to see Uncle Gaige last night because I like the idea of having someone on staff who has a social work background. I wondered if that would also lend itself to teaching."

Hadleigh cocked her head to the side. "Teaching in what capacity?"

Emmy giggled. "We have kids on the two compounds. You've met Callie and Anders. But my Uncle Gaige has an eighteen-month-old, Tate. Wyatt and Yvette are expecting a baby. Jax and Dodge have eighteen-month-old twins. Axel and Bridget have Aidyn who is six now. And, I'll bet it won't be long before Josh and Isi have a baby of their own and then there's the team here. Then Ford and Megan have Shelby, though they are off-site. So are Jax and Dodge, but they bring the kids here for school. Eventually most or all of us will have kids. Because of the nature of our jobs, we homeschool the kids because we can't risk kidnapping. There is always someone wanting to get even. It's a fact of our jobs. Between Bridget, Yvette, my Aunt Sophie, and Skye, the kids are pretty well rounded as far as how they are taught and what they are taught. But someone with social work experience would sure be nice. There are times when the kids that come to us, such as Callie and Anders, need a bit of support in life after a trauma. That's where you come in. So, between that support and teaching I think we can keep you busy and pay you for that as well."

"That would be amazing." Hadleigh smiled, her heartbeat increasing.

"So, Skye Montgomery used to be in HR before she and Lincoln married. Since then, she's become invaluable for GHOST and now for RAPTOR. She'll work up the job description and duties and go over all of this with you in more detail. I'll ask her to give you a call."

Hadleigh swallowed the emotion in her throat. "Thank you, Emmy. Really, thank you."

Emmy smiled and stood. "Thank you Hadleigh. We'll all be better for the relationship I think."

Hadleigh left the office, excited about the future. Donovan said he'd wait for her upstairs, and Hadleigh was grateful she had the time to process her conversation with Emmy.

When she opened the door to Donovan's apartment, the first thing she saw was a huge bouquet of red roses sitting on the coffee table in a crystal vase. A card stuck out of the side of the bouquet and she saw her name written in scrawling cursive. It had a capital H on it and the gh at the end seemed to be her name. The squiggly line in between was anyone's bet.

She opened the card and read, "Congratulations, you deserve it. XOXOXO"

Tears sprang to her eyes as she looked around for Donovan. On the coffee table lay a white envelope with her name scrawled across it. She picked it up and read, "I'm in the garage."

Her brows wrinkled but she bent to smell the perfume of the roses, then left the apartment to find Van.

She skipped down the steps, excitement coursing through her body to tell him the news. Exiting through the hallway, she opened the garage door but didn't see or hear anyone. As a matter of fact, most of the vehicles were gone. Turning the corner toward Van's rented SUV, she caught sight of him leaning against the back of it, his arms crossed over his chest and a big smile on his handsome face.

"Hi." She greeted.

He stepped toward her, his smile growing as he neared. "Hi."

He leaned down and kissed her lips, his soft and full and molding to hers perfectly.

"I'm now a RAPTOR employee."

"I know."

"How do you know?"

"Emmy called me last night; you were sleeping. She wanted to make sure we were solid before bringing you on. She had no worries about you doing your job, she worried that if we weren't solid, it would or could affect the team."

Hadleigh's smile grew. "You said we were solid?"

"MmmHmm."

"Oh, I love hearing that."

"Good. Let's go for a ride."

Her brows bunched again, "Where to?"

He chuckled, "You'll see."

He helped her into the vehicle, drove out of the garage and onto the street. He was secretive but smiling.

When he turned onto her street, she was surprised and looked between Van and her house as they approached. Nothing looked out of place. Nothing seemed different.

"What is going on here?"

He merely chuckled.

Van pulled into her driveway and immediately exited the vehicle. He walked around the front of the SUV and opened her door. Holding his hand out for her to take, he bowed slightly at the waist, "Madam."

She laughed. "Sir."

Whatever he had planned it was starting to be fun.

He walked her to the front door, unlocked it with a set of keys that she recognized as her own. "How did you get..."

He pushed open the door and the floral aroma that wafted from the living room was amazing.

She stepped into the room and saw flowers on every surface of the room. Roses in various colors, red, yellow, white, coral. Daisies, carnations, spider mums in various colors.

"Oh my word, this is just amazing." She looked at him and saw his smile, then continued to look at all the flowers.

She turned to look at him again and he was on one knee.

"I wasn't sure what kind of flowers you loved most, but Emmy and Charly told me roses are always a safe bet. What I knew is that you are more beautiful than any flower on earth. When you look at a flower, you see it's outward beauty—the color, the shape of it. But, the inside of the flower, the aroma, the way it feeds bees and other things that are needed to pollinate and feed other flowers and birds, that's the part people don't always appreciate or think of. When I look at you, I see the outside beauty, everyone does. You're absolutely stunning. But what they don't get to see, that I have seen, is your inside beauty. You love and care for children. You love people and want to always see them for the good and not the bad. That's your aroma Hadleigh. You'll always be my rose. I always want to be in your presence and enjoy your beauty and bask in your aroma. Will you marry me, Hadleigh and let me care for you for all of my days?"

She stared at him, stunned. This was so out of the blue and yet so romantic. So, pure and thoughtful, she'd never have dreamed anything like this for a proposal.

"Yes." It came out as a whisper because tears clogged her throat. She nodded her head vigorously to emphasize her acceptance and saw him visibly relax before standing and taking her into his arms and holding her tightly. He rained kisses on her head, her cheeks, her lips, finally her lips.

When they parted and he set her down, she giggled. "How did you do all of this? I was only with Emmy for less than an hour."

"Well, I have eight team members, a team member spouse, and two kids eager to help."

He took her hand and walked her to the sliding patio doors to her back yard. He opened the doors and announced, "She said, yes."

His teammates began cheering as they came out from behind shrubs and her garden shed in the back yard. She stood staring in disbelief at the feelings that washed through her as she was accepted into this amazing organization.

Van turned to her. "Before you get mobbed, I want you to know you've made me incredibly happy."

She laughed, "Oh my God, you have made me so happy and I'm stunned. Truly, stunned. Also, I don't see any reason for a long engagement, do you?"

***

Did you notice the sparks flying between Charly and Sam? Read their story in Craving Charlesia.

EPILOGUE

Van slapped Charly's hands away from his tie, for the fourth time. "Stop fussing."

"Well, you keep messing it up."

"It's fine, Charly."

She shrugged, her blond curls bobbing, "Fine. But I'm telling Hadleigh I tried to make you look perfect and you kept fidgeting and messing up your tie."

Van laughed. "I'll tell Bowers you have a huge ass crush on him if you do."

"I don't have a crush on him. The man just happens to be the perfect specimen of your gender and I enjoy looking at him."

"Crush."

"Not."

Deacon walked over to them, "Stop arguing. The congregation can hear you two."

Charly placed her hands on her hips and stared straight into Deacon's eyes.

"We're not that loud."

"You are and I agree with Van, you've got a hot-ass, larger than life, honest to God, crush on Bowers."

Charly's lips thinned but she said nothing. After a moment of everyone wondering if she were going to haul off and smack Deacon, she instead turned and walked away.

"I'm going down by the women, who by the way, agree with me." She walked a few steps before turning and landing a sharp-eyed gaze at Van, "Including Hadleigh."

Before he could respond, she was gone.

Van straightened his shoulders and looked at Deacon. "Perfect specimen my ass."

Deacon laughed. "Big galoot if you ask me."

Van nodded and turned when the door to the rectory room opened and the minister stepped in.

"I see you're ready to get married. I'm told the women are now ready after fussing at the doorway as some of the congregation walked in. It appears they are into the male form, particularly one man."

"For God's sake." Van spewed.

The minister cleared his throat and shook his head.

"I mean, for Fu..."

More head shaking and finally a save as Diego walked over and put a hand on Van's shoulder. "Just let it be, man."

Falcon laughed across the room as did Deacon, Caiden and Creed. Diego shook his head as he smiled.

"Okay, it seems I better go get married before Bowers comes in and takes Hadleigh away."

Caiden shook his head, "You got it bad, man."

"Fu..." He looked at the minister. Holding his hand down low, he shot Caiden the finger which earned him laughs from everyone.

The minister, clearly not enjoying the moment, cleared his throat. "Places, please."

The men walked out of the rector's office and down a back hallway to meet their bridesmaids to escort them down the aisle. Except for Van, who walked out with the minister to stand at the front of the church.

Hadleigh's mother had been gone for years; her father had been a football coach in his prime. He now tended to his yard, watched all the football on television he could stomach, walked two miles every day and looked fit as a fiddle. He had granted his permission after Van had asked him in a quick phone call before he actually proposed.

The music began with the songs he and Hadleigh had selected. He didn't care what was played while they married; Hadleigh had some must-haves, and he eagerly agreed. The couples, one by one, walked down the aisle. His friends and co-workers all chuckled and looked at Van as they walked past Bowers, much to Van's irritation. No way to flip them off now. He'd have to do it later.

Finally, Diego and Shelby, their best man and matron of honor, took their places and the music changed and the volume rose as Hadleigh and her father appeared in the doorway at the back of the church.

Van's throat constricted as he watched his beautiful bride float down the aisle toward him. She was stunning in her white gown, speckled with crystals that glittered with each step. The smile on her face was perfection and he smirked when she floated past Bowers and didn't pay a single bit of attention to him. As they neared the steps, Van stepped down, and shook his soon-to-be father-in-law's hand.

"Thank you for granting me the honor of marrying your daughter, sir."

Dax Watterson, smiled at Van, and looked him in the eye. "You're welcome. You and I will have some unpleasant conversations if you ever make her unhappy, son."

Van smiled. "Yes sir."

Dax turned and kissed his daughter's cheek, then wrapped her in a warm embrace.

"Your mother is with us today, baby girl. She's so proud of you, as am I."

"Thank you, Daddy." Hadleigh whispered.

Dax stepped away and stood at the end of the front pew in the church and Hadleigh moved toward Van. He extended his arm to her and she slid hers into the crook of his elbow. They walked up the two steps to the altar and faced the minister.

hey shared their first meal together as husband and wife. They laughed. They had their first dance, of many, as husband and wife. They enjoyed celebrating with their friends and family. The evening was spectacular. And as they started saying their good-byes for the night, they were tired.

Charly and Emmy were huddled together in a corner, and soon Piper, Falcon, and Creed joined them. Van noticed the huddle and he and Hadleigh walked over to see what was going on.

"Hey, what's up?" Van asked.

Emmy looked up at him, "Van, we don't want to intrude on your wedding."

"Don't shut us out, it'll only bother both of us."

Hadleigh nodded in agreement.

Charly turned. "Remember Olive Tomms?"

"Of course, how could I ever forget her?" Van turned to Hadleigh, "Olive is one of the three kids we saved just before we quit our jobs with Operation Live Again."

"Oh, okay."

Charly continued. "Olive's sister, Haylie, was also kidnapped at the same time and Olive is now missing again."

Emmy looked at Van. "I'm sending Charly, Falcon, and Diego to find both of them."

"Where are their parents for fucks' sake?"

Emmy shook her head, "Both are addicts. The girls have been left to their own devices for years."

Hadleigh asked, "Where is social services in this instance?"

Emmy shrugged. "I don't know, Hadleigh. But, when you get back from your honeymoon, hopefully we'll have the girls and you will be called on to help them out."

"I'll be ready and if you need us to come back early, just call." She turned to Van, "Agreed?"

His heart swelled; she was just like a rose. "I do agree."

Emmy turned to her team members. "Okay, Cyber, let's pull files together. Get all the information from the dark web you can. Caiden, you'll need to man the new software and get it working for us. There must be traces of these girls out there. Especially Olive, since she was involved with us previously. We have photos, fingerprints, etcetera. Let's pull it all together so Charly, Diego, and Falcon have something to go on. Deacon and Creed, you focus on Haylie Tomms. Gather all her information, last places seen, activities, schools, a full workup."

Everyone nodded their agreement—RAPTOR was on another mission. This one was close to their hearts.

Read all about it in Craving Charlesia.

ALSO BY PJ FIALA

Click here to see a list of all of my books with the blurbs.

Contemporary Romance
Rolling Thunder Series
Moving to Love, Book 1

Moving to Hope, Book 2

Moving to Forever, Book 3

Moving to Desire, Book 4

Moving to You, Book 5

Moving Home, Book 6

Moving On, Book 7

Rolling Thunder Boxset, Books 1-4

Military Romantic Suspense
Second Chances Series
Designing Samantha's Love, Book 1

Securing Kiera's Love, Book 2

Second Chances Boxset - Duet

Bluegrass Security Series
Heart Thief, Book One

Finish Line, Book Two

Lethal Love, Book Three

Bluegrass Security Boxset, Books 1-3

Big 3 Security

Ford: Finding His Fire Book One

Lincoln: Finding His Mark Book Two

Dodge: Finding His Jewel Book Three

Rory: Finding His Match Book Four

Big 3 Security Boxset, Books 1-4

GHOST

Defending Keirnan, GHOST Book One

Defending Sophie, GHOST Book Two

Defending Roxanne, GHOST Book Three

Defending Yvette, GHOST Book Four

Defending Bridget, GHOST Book Five

Defending Isabella, GHOST Book Six

RAPTOR

RAPTOR Rising - Prequel

Saving Shelby, RAPTOR Book One

Holding Hadleigh, RAPTOR Book Two

Craving Charlesia, RAPTOR Book Three

Promising Piper, RAPTOR Book Four

Missing Mia, RAPTOR Book Five

Believing Becca, RAPTOR Book Six

Keeping Kori, RAPTOR Book Seven

Healing Hope, RAPTOR Book Eight

Engaging Emersyn, RAPTOR Book Nine

MEET PJ

Writing has been a desire my whole life. Once I found the courage to write, life changed for me in the most profound way. Bringing stories to readers that I'd enjoy reading and creating characters that are flawed, but lovable is such a joy.

When not writing, I'm with my family doing something fun. My husband, Gene, and I are bikers and enjoy riding to new locations, meeting new people and generally enjoying this fabulous country we live in.

I come from a family of veterans. My grandfather, father, brother, two sons, and one daughter-in-law are all veterans. Needless to say, I am proud to be an American and proud of the service my amazing family has given.

My online home is https://www.pjfiala.com.
You can connect with me on Facebook at https://www.facebook.com/PJFiala1,

and
Instagram at https://www.Instagram.com/PJFiala.
If you prefer to email, go ahead, I'll respond -
pjfiala@pjfiala.com.

Made in the USA
Monee, IL
23 September 2022